THE HIGHWAYMAN'S HIDDEN HEART(ONLY FOR LOVE BOOK 5)

A CLEAN REGENCY ROMANCE

ROSE PEARSON

LANDON HILL MEDIA

THE HIGHWAYMAN'S
HIDDEN HEART

PROLOGUE

Felix Millshaw, Viscount Winterbrook, sighed heavily.

"It is all so very dull, is it not?"

His friend widened his eyes. The ball was in full flow and all around them, there was conversation and laughter – seemingly a perfectly excellent evening for any gentleman to enjoy.

"Good gracious, whatever is the matter, Winterbrook? Are you a little frustrated that Lady Perla has not come to speak with you?" Lord Bramwell's lips curved a little. "You *are* aware that, on occasion, you must remove yourself from your chair and go in search of the young lady of your interest, rather than waiting for her to come to you."

"I am well aware of that." Felix did not give in to Lord Bramwell's gentle mocking, finding himself a little frustrated at his friend's remarks. "The reason I remain in my chair is because I do not wish to speak with any young lady, and I certainly have no desire to dance."

Lord Bramwell looked at him as though he had gone quite mad, his features creasing as he squinted.

"You do not wish to dance? Even though you are at a ball?"

"No." Felix shrugged. "I do not wish to."

"And whyever not? This is your third Season. Surely you must now be all too aware of what a gentleman can enjoy in the Season?"

Sighing, Felix shook his head.

"Alas, that may be so, but I am unfortunately disinclined to the idea of doing exactly the same thing, year upon year. I am becoming a little tired of it."

His friend frowned, clearly having very little comprehension of what Felix was speaking about.

With a frown of his own, Felix tried again.

"It is all the same." Felix held out one hand, gesturing to the ball going on around them. "It is all just as you see here. Every Season I come to London. I take part in the various balls, soirees, dinners, et cetera with the same smiles, the same welcomes, the same expectations... and I find myself becoming a little bored with it. There is nothing new. There is no real excitement. How can a gentleman find his Season to be of any joy when it is nothing but familiarity?"

Lord Bramwell's mouth fell open, and Felix sighed and looked away. It was clear that his friend had very little understanding of what Felix was trying to say, and he was uncertain of whether he wished to make the effort to further explain himself. After all, he had been thinking about this for some time, and had chased after the usual pursuits – gambling, cards, and the like – and had found himself still filled with ennui in the face of it all.

"This is beyond my understanding."

"That is because you do not see it, I think." Searching for words, he tried to express the restlessness in his soul, the heaviness of his heart as he looked upon the same faces, felt the same anticipations, and found very little of interest in either. "You seek pleasure. You dance with many a young lady and tangle with some, while I grow weary of it all."

"Then you must be thinking of matrimony, for surely marriage is the desire of every gentleman at some point in his life?"

Felix rolled his eyes.

"You sound like my dearest Mama. Yes, I am aware that there is a requirement to marry. I have been aware of it ever since I came into the title at so young an age, but I will not confess myself eager to do it. If I find society dull and staid, then will I not find my wife – whomever she may be – similar in every way? Every day of every year, she will remain the same and I shall drown in ennui. I shall find myself in an even worse situation than I am at present!" He shook his head. "No, there must be more to life than this, to simply having responsibilities throughout the year and in the Season, having a few moments of respite from them all. If I am to enjoy the same pleasures, in the same company, at the same events, as I do every year then no, my friend, I do not have the same enjoyment as you during this London Season. There is too much familiarity. There is no excitement in anything. There must be something more to this."

Lord Bramwell shook his head, his fingers running over his jaw.

"You sound very strange indeed, my friend."

"Then you do not understand."

"No, I do not." Lord Bramwell shrugged, then gestured to the ballroom. "When I look out at this, I see nothing *but* excitement. I do not find anything to be overly familiar. Indeed, I make certain that those I dance with have very little in common with those I have seen the previous Season. It takes a little effort, but I find even the effort itself to be worthwhile. Perhaps that is where you are lacking. Mayhap you are becoming a little lazy."

He grinned but Felix did not smile. Yet again, Lord Bramwell showed an entire lack of clarity when it came to this. How could he explain something to someone who could not understand? And how could he do so when he was struggling to make sense of it himself?

"You speak of matrimony," he said quickly, thinking to put the focus back upon his friend. "Does that mean that *you* are considering finding yourself a bride?"

He had thought his remark would make Lord Bramwell pull back from the conversation but, much to his astonishment, Lord Bramwell shrugged.

"Mayhap I am in a mind to do so. I find myself considering it, at the very least, and no, do not hide your surprise at my statement. I have no intention of hiding such a thing from you. You may very well find me courting this Season, with the intention of securing a bride."

Felix blinked.

"Truly?"

Lord Bramwell nodded and there was a small smile on his face which Felix could not understand. How could his friend appear so contented with the idea?

"Indeed. If I find a suitable young lady then I might indeed find myself drawing near the altar – but now, let us consider you again." His friend smiled quietly, no longer grinning. "Yes, I am aware that you sought to speak of my situation so that we did not need to discuss yours, but I am not as willing to forget about what you have said as you might desire."

Grimacing, Felix shrugged.

"There is very little point in discussing it."

"Come now," his friend retorted. "There must be something which can be done, something which will lift your spirits. Have you thought of nothing which might chase away this melancholy?"

Felix managed a small smile, although he did not look in Lord Bramwell's direction, curiously perturbed by his friend's remark as regarded matrimony.

"You need not concern yourself. Yes, I have considered, and I have some plans afoot for what I shall do to enliven things."

There came a short silence. Felix caught the lift of his friend's eyebrow but chose to say nothing more. With a frustrated breath, Lord Bramwell threw up his hands.

"And you will not tell me what these plans are? You are determined to keep them hidden?"

Tilting his head, Felix hesitated.

"I think it only wise to keep such things from you, my friend. You have shown an inclination to a loose tongue on occasion."

Lord Bramwell laughed.

"Alas, you have injured me!" His eyes twinkled. "Well, whatever endeavors it is you pursue, I hope you find them to be a good deal more intriguing than your life here in society."

Felix nodded, speaking both to himself and his friend.

"I have every hope that it will be."

CHAPTER ONE

"And are you looking forward to the Season, my dear? It is certain to be an excellent one, I am sure."

Lady Elizabeth gave her mother a small smile as the carriage made its way to London.

"Yes, Mama."

It was the required response, and Elizabeth knew precisely what her mother was hoping for this coming Season. Thus far, in her previous two Seasons, she had danced and conversed and walked with various gentlemen but, as yet, had not found a suitable gentleman who wished to court her. One or two gentlemen had asked to court her, but she had refused them, simply because she had found the gentlemen who had asked such things of her to be entirely disagreeable. She and her friends had, together, sworn that they should only marry for love, and that they would support each other in their endeavors. Therefore, with their pact remaining strong, Elizabeth had every confidence that she would find a suitable gentleman, regardless of how long it took her.

"Mayhap you need to give up this idea." As though she

had known what Elizabeth was thinking, her mother chimed into Elizabeth's thoughts. "You made it quite clear from the very beginning that only a particular circumstance would please you. However, I am not certain that such a thing is wise."

"I see."

This was accepted with nothing more than a brief murmur. It would be best, Elizabeth considered, to allow her mother to continue on in such a vein if she wished. She was all too aware that her mother desired her to wed, and to wed very soon if she could. Indeed, to be on one's third Season without even a courtship was a little embarrassing in some regards, but Elizabeth did not allow it to concern her. Her resolve was steady. She had a somewhat quiet nature, but her determination was strong – much to the chagrin of her mother!

"Perhaps you might consider a kind gentleman only," Lady Longford continued quickly. "A *kind* gentleman will soon fall in love with you. Although he may not do it initially, it would come after your wedding day. That would be suitable, would it not?"

Elizabeth arched a gentle eyebrow in her mother's direction.

"Mama, I am well aware that my determination in this matter is not something you are used to. I know that both of my elder sisters married gentlemen that you and father proposed for them - gentlemen who are kind and generous, as you have suggested for me. They are also wealthy and well-titled which, again, must please you and father very much." Her resolve to remain silent faded quickly, she threw up her hands. "I, however, will *not* be the same. I understand your concern for me, but if I am to do without love, then I would rather become a spinster and care for my sisters' children. I would rather that life than find myself married to a gentleman who did not love me. Besides which, Mama, kindness does not mean that a gentleman has any real capacity for love. It would not be guaranteed, and I would not take the risk."

Warmth grew in her cheeks as she realized that she had spoken very openly indeed, instead of remaining silent, as she had first resolved to do. Her mother frowned, her sharp eyes searching Elizabeth's face as if she were displeased with her, perhaps frustrated that Elizabeth was being so stubborn. Again, however, Elizabeth did not find her mother's consideration of her to be particularly burdensome. Her mother was always going to be this way, encouraging her to do the opposite of what Elizabeth had determined to do because she wished to see her daughter wed. It was a somewhat difficult conundrum. How could a mother love her children but, at the same time, have her only desire be for them to marry, regardless of their own considerations? At times, particularly as she had watched the situation with her older sisters, it seemed as though a mother's only interest was to make certain that her daughters were wed to *any* suitable gentlemen. It was as if the state of marriage was more important than her daughter's happiness.

But I shall not allow that to be so for me.

"There is Lord Newport, I suppose." Elizabeth closed her eyes. "He is handsome, *very* charming, has a great deal of wealth, and owns a large estate up in Scotland, from what I understand." Biting her lip, Elizabeth forced her response back, swallowing her words. "He was interested in you last Season, although you did not seem to return his interest."

"That is because I had no interest in him." Speaking rather swiftly, Elizabeth tried to retain some composure.

"Mama, Lord Newport is an older gentleman, closer in age to you and Papa than to me."

Her mother folded her hands in her lap, one eyebrow lifting.

"But what would that matter, if he claimed to love you?"

The challenge in her words gave Elizabeth pause. She did not like the way that her mother continued to question her. It seemed as if she wanted to tie her up with chains of her own words.

"I must fall in love with the gentleman also. Surely you can understand why I have no consideration for Lord Newport, Mama! From my point of view, the only thing that he desires is a young bride on his arm. That is all, nothing more. He does not care for me, not in the least."

"I do think it a little unfair of you to judge him so." Sighing heavily, and with obvious discontent, her mother looked out of the window as the carriage trundled along. "Well then, if you are not to marry Lord Newport, would you consider Lord Greenfield?"

A flicker of anger threatened, and Elizabeth sucked in a breath, turning her attention to the countryside outside rather than answering Lady Longford. How long would she have to endure her mother's encouragement in this matter? They had been in the carriage for some four days now, broken up by various visits to inns and the like but, the closer they came to London, the more eager her mother became. Even though her previous resolve had failed her, Elizabeth set her shoulders and kept her gaze at the window. This time, she determined, she would not look at her mother, nor listen to what she had to say. She would let her words wash over her like the rain, brushing down over her skin but without making any real impact. Lady Longford could suggest all the gentlemen she wished, but that did not mean that Elizabeth would be in any way affected by her ideas. Tilting her chin up, Elizabeth gritted her teeth as Lady Longford continued to describe the achievements of Lord Greenfield - a gentleman who was so full of his own appearance, he did nothing but gaze at himself in any looking glass or reflection he could find!

To remain silent until we reach London will be a very difficult challenge indeed!

~

Elizabeth did not know how long Lady Longford had spoken. She was drifting somewhere between being lost in thought and weariness - tired from the journey, tired from the banality of her drive, but most of all, weary of her mother's conversation. She had droned on and on about the various gentlemen Elizabeth might consider while Elizabeth had said nothing whatsoever, and had given only the occasional murmur to indicate that she was still paying attention when, of course, she had been doing her very best to ignore her mother's every word.

"Oh, and we must not forget Lord Pickett!"

Inwardly recoiling, Elizabeth turned to look at her mother again. Lord Pickett was a fop, and she would do nothing to encourage his attentions.

"Mama, I am aware that there are many gentlemen who may wish to court me, but you must recall that *I* may not –"

Her resolve to remain silent was broken, but her sentence thereafter was cut short by a sudden, harsh cry which was quickly met by a shout from their coachman. The horses whinnied and the carriage slowed abruptly and with such fierceness that it threw Elizabeth and her mother off their seat.

It took Elizabeth a few moments to gather herself again, realizing that she was somewhere between the floor and the seat opposite her. Blinking, she pushed herself back to her previous position, immediately looking at her mother, who had one hand pressed to her forehead and was now very pale indeed.

"Whatever happened?" Her eyes took in the whiteness of her mother's face, and she grasped her hand, her irritation forgotten. "Are you quite all right?"

"I am a little pained." The slight quaver to Lady Longford's voice had Elizabeth's concern growing rapidly. When her mother took her hand away from her forehead, there was a large bruise and a lump on her forehead – a bruise that was already darkening. "I do not know what I hit my head on, but it is painful." Lady Longford winced. "Why ever did we stop so?"

"I do not know."

Elizabeth, who was herself nursing a few bruises, looked out of the window and then made to rap on the roof for their coachman. She could not understand why they had stopped so rapidly, nor why the coachman had behaved with such evident inconsideration. Her hand fell back when another bout of shouting rang around outside them and, to her utter astonishment, a face appeared at the window.

With a shriek, Elizabeth fell back against the squabs as her mother moved away as best as she could, scrabbling into the corner of the carriage. The face - or what Elizabeth could see of it - was that of a man who was, strangely, smiling broadly at them both. His eyes were hidden behind a mask of sorts, the type she might expect to see upon a gentleman at a masquerade ball. Dark eyes glinted behind it with a few dark curls poking out from either side of his hat. Fear gripped her, her heart pounding so fiercely that she was afraid it might leap from her chest.

"No need to be afraid." His voice was a little muffled by the window, but his meaning became all too clear when he tapped on the window with his pistol. Elizabeth let out another shriek as the man, opened the door himself, playing the part of a footman, and let down the steps. With a flourish, he bowed low, then stood with one arm stretched out towards her. "Good afternoon. Allow me to escort you from the carriage."

Taking in a deep breath, Elizabeth looked first to her mother and then back to the highwayman. Lady Longford was shaking, huddled in the corner of the carriage, her face turned away from the man who now stood before them. Elizabeth had no doubt of what he was, having heard stories about men such as these. They preyed upon carriages, no doubt quite certain that ladies and gentlemen of wealth would be making their way to London... but never had she thought that her own carriage would be caught by such a nefarious person.

Then I must be bold and refuse to allow my fears to take hold.

"As you can see," she began, hearing the tremble in her voice, "my mother is not well enough to be removed from the carriage." Lady Longford dared to turn her head, then let out a shriek before burrowing it back into the carriage seat again. "For her sake, you must let us be on our way at once."

The man laughed, his eyes twinkling as though the remark were some sort of great joke that he was now thoroughly enjoying.

"I am afraid that I am not the one to be commanded, my Lady." He gestured to Lady Longford with his pistol free hand. "I can, of course, see that your mother is rather afraid of the circumstances, but nonetheless that will not prevent me from taking my gains from you."

Elizabeth drew herself up, ignoring the hammering of her heart. She had no choice but to be forthright, had no option but to be courageous, for who else in the situation was to be so? She could not think of her mother, for she was already terrified and weeping, and given the pistol in the highwayman's hand, Elizabeth did admit to being fearful for their safety.

"*I* will step down from the carriage." Lifting her chin, she clasped her hands tightly together so that he would not notice them shaking. "And because I have done as you bid me, you will leave my mother as she is."

The highwayman's smile slipped a little.

"You show a good deal of spirit, my Lady."

"Will it be enough to satisfy you?" she challenged, refusing to remove from her seat until he had agreed to her request. "Leave my mother as she is."

"You are also a very obstinate young lady." The gentleman waved his pistol around freely as he gestured. "But I fear that I have no other choice but to agree. Yes, my Lady, so long as you remove yourself from the carriage, I shall leave your mother as she is."

Elizabeth glanced at her mother again, but Lady Longford did not so much as turn her head. Finally, praying that she would not end up dead because of her courage, Elizabeth made her way from the carriage, horrified when the gentleman put out his hand, and she had no other choice but to take it, to assist her to step down. To grasp the hand of a highwayman who was surely an evil fellow was almost a wickedness in itself!

"Very well."

Standing in front of her carriage, Elizabeth tilted her head, looking back at the highwayman – only to catch her breath in horror as she realized that he, standing there with a pistol, was not alone, but was accompanied by three other highwaymen. They remained on their horses, one on either side of the coachman, with the third in front of the horses, holding the bridle of the lead horse. How relieved she was now that her mother had been permitted to remain in the carriage! Had she stepped outside, Elizabeth had every belief that she would have fainted with shock.

"Might I say that you are as beautiful as a summer's morning, my Lady."

The highwayman's smooth manner and confident speech had her curling her lip.

"I am not about to be taken in by any flirtations." Looking the highwayman straight in the eye, she put her hands on her hips. "I have no dreams of being flattered and fawned over by a highwayman. You wish to steal from me, is that not so? You wish to take what does not belong to you and take it solely for yourself, so that you need not work for your keep, as so many others are required to."

There was, again, a slight tremble in her voice, but she ignored it, holding his gaze steadily and catching how his lips pulled into a small smile. She shivered lightly.

"You may consider me as you wish." The highwayman shrugged, looking at her keenly, his eyes mysterious, hidden from her. "Yet regardless of what you wish, I shall still be taking something valuable from you. How else am I to pay my men?" Grinning, he glanced at his companions, one of whom chuckled as Elizabeth looked away.

"Very well then, *sir*." Putting as much irony into her address of him as she could, she spread out both hands. "What is it you shall have from me?"

CHAPTER TWO

Felix grinned to himself. This young woman, whoever she was, was the most extraordinary creature he had ever come across. She was beautiful, of course, for what young lady of London was not beautiful in some way? It was her spirit, however, which was utterly remarkable. He was quite sure that he had never come across such a person before, for what young lady of quality would dare stand up to a highwayman? What strength it took for her to speak to him in the manner and tone which she had done! Everyone else he had ever stopped had cowered in fear before him. Some had trembled, and one or two had even fainted. Any young lady he had come across had always remained hidden in her carriage, silent and afraid until, at last, she had been forced to step out. He had never demanded much from any of them, for gaining wealth was not his purpose in doing such things. It was all a little jest on his part, at least. He paid the three rogues handsomely for coming along with him, out of his own pocket, but whatever he took, he always found a way of returning. Yes, everyone he held up was upset and displeased with him, but he did not care about their consideration of him. That was not his purpose here. His only purpose was to find a little enjoyment - and what enjoyment he was having at this moment!

"Well?" The young woman sighed heavily as if he was wasting her time. "What is it that you intend to take from me? You have said nothing for some minutes, and I confess I am a little frustrated!"

Felix chuckled. Taking a small step closer, he regarded her carefully, tipping his head from one side to the other and allowing his gaze to traverse slowly from the ground at her feet to the very top of her head. To her credit, the young lady did not so much as flinch, nor did she even blush. Instead, her flashing blue eyes regarded him sharply, her lips thin as though daring him to make a single remark about his study. Gentle brown curls danced lightly in the breeze, the sun lending it a sweet copper tone and Felix found his smile growing. Obviously, the young lady was not at all appreciative of the silence, but he had no desire to hurry through this moment. He was enjoying himself far too much.

"I will tell you, my Lady, that I do not think I have ever met anyone with as much gumption as you."

The young lady sighed and shook her head.

"I am afraid that gumption is not a trait which young ladies are particularly well known for." Her arms were folded across her chest, her eyes as sharp as shards of glass. "And still, you have not answered my question. If you seek to compliment me to ease my current difficulties, then I can assure you it will mean nothing to me. I would rather let you take from me what you wish, and then let us be on our way."

"But you would deny me the pleasure of your company

for a little longer?" Felix held out both hands in an almost begging fashion. "And what if I were to suggest that a prolonged conversation with me might make me consider leaving you with all that you currently have?"

Her eyes closed and she let out a little huff.

"I should not like, at all, to be in your company for any duration. Instead, I would much prefer to give you *more* than you asked for, rather than spend even a single minute of my time furthering our acquaintance."

Her words were so cutting that Felix did not immediately respond, such was his surprise. Every young lady of his acquaintance thus far had always been very careful to speak with as much decorum as they ought. This young lady, however, seemed to have no quibble, no hesitation, in speaking precisely as she wished, and Felix admitted silently to admiring it.

"I see that you do not hold your tongue either, as might be expected from a young lady," he remarked, as the young lady frowned, her mouth in a tight line. "Very well, very well. I shall not force my company upon you. Instead, however, I will simply take the brooch which you wear upon your traveling cloak and, thereafter, permit your coachman to drive you, and your mother, away. I assume that you are going to London?" Chuckling, he smiled broadly. "I doubt we shall ever meet again."

That, of course, was quite a lie, for Felix had every intention of seeking this lady out again, albeit without his highwayman garb.

"My – my brooch?" The young woman blinked. Her hand lifted to the brooch, and the courage he had admired seemed to fade as her fingers traced across it. It was not overly large but had one purple sapphire within it, surrounded by diamonds. "You would take a family heirloom from me?" Her face crumpled, her lips pulling down, her eyes closing, gentle lines crossing her forehead and, for a moment he thought she was going to beseech him, only for her to turn her head away. Many a young lady had cried when he had come upon them, but this young woman's tears seemed to mean a great deal more to him. He had never allowed himself to feel guilty, but this young lady's glassy eyes were stabbing him with shame. "Very well."

Much to Felix's surprise, the young lady unpinned it from her traveling cloak and, with it clenched tightly in her hand, stepped forward, holding it out to him. Her eyes were still a little red-rimmed but, all the same, she held his gaze steadily and did not flinch.

"I have the feeling that this brooch means a great deal to you." Felix held out his open hand and after only a moment, she dropped the brooch into it. "A family heirloom, you say? Does not every young lady have more than one piece such as this?"

She looked somewhere over his shoulder, seemingly no longer willing to look into his eyes.

"Alas, I am the youngest of three daughters. I have been given one valuable piece and *only* one. It belonged to my grandmother. She wore it on the day of her wedding." Her eyes darted to his for just a moment as though she had hoped to find sympathy in his expression, but was immediately disappointed. "But then again, I suppose a highwayman would not care about the memories such a thing holds, nor understand the significance of a single item."

She went to turn away, to go back to her carriage, and Felix, much to his astonishment, grasped her wrist. When she turned back to face him, he surprised himself all the more by stepping forward, dropping his head, and pressing a kiss to her lips.

To his amazement, the young lady did not step back. She did not pull herself away, nor strike out at him and then hurry off into her carriage. Instead, she remained precisely as she was, although mostly, he considered, her nearness to him came from the shock of his action rather than from any enjoyment. With a sigh of contentment, he broke their kiss but remained close to her, looking down into her eyes, and seeing how wide they were. Grinning to himself at how much he had managed to change her expression, he shrugged lightly.

"Mayhap a kiss will take the place of the memories this brooch holds."

The young lady blinked, her face flooding with color before she wrenched her hand away from his. Her feet took her directly back to her carriage and, not allowing himself to linger, Felix climbed back upon his horse, and with a wave to his men, rode away from the carriage. He turned his head for a moment and looked back at the young lady. She had not climbed into the safety of the carriage as he had expected but was instead standing beside it, one hand on the door, her eyes locked upon him. He could not imagine what she was thinking. No doubt she was very angry with him indeed, and deeply upset at the loss of her brooch, but Felix did not allow himself to ponder any rising guilt. He would return the brooch to her somehow, for it was not the value of the items he craved. Rather, it was the excitement, the anticipation, the sheer enjoyment of riding wild, of stopping those making their way to London, and engaging with their reactions.

Certainly, I was not disappointed with this particular young lady!

The wind in his face, Felix allowed himself a broad smile. She had been the most delightful company. Even though she had been displeased with what he had done, he had enjoyed every moment of being with her. The kiss had been entirely unplanned but, all the same, he had reveled in it. Turning his head away and urging his horse forward, he allowed his thoughts to linger on the young lady, realizing that he had not discovered her name.

That was to be his task, then. Once he was returned to being a gentleman of society, he would make it his task to find the young lady again and obtain an introduction to her.

"It appears to me as though you have been a little more contented these last few days."

Felix looked at Lord Bramwell sidelong, then shrugged.

"Mayhap I am," he answered, giving no real explanation for why such a thing might be. "Or mayhap I am simply putting on a show for you, so that you will not complain about my dulled spirits."

Lord Bramwell chuckled.

"You know as well as I, that would not work." He lifted his chin. "I can always tell when you playact, given that we have known each other for so long. In truth, since we are almost always in company during the Season, I believe that I can tell precisely how you are feeling and whether or not you put on a pretense." Tipping his head, he smiled, his eyes glinting. "So you may as well tell me the truth."

Felix shook his head. That was the last thing he was about to do. He could not exactly confess to his friend that, on occasion, he became a highwayman, and therefore, some of his days were spent on the outskirts of London, trying to find as many carriages and unsuspecting ladies and gentlemen as he could.

"I will not tell you, I am afraid."

"Then it must be a lady."

Lord Bramwell nudged him hard, and Felix laughed, seeing his friend grin.

"Is that so?"

"Yes, because you do not want to tell me the truth. Therefore, I am certain it is a young woman who has captured your attention. In recognizing this, you now are at a loss about what to do, even though you are a good deal more contented." Lord Bramwell turned so that he faced Felix straight on, blocking out his sight of the ladies and gentlemen as they danced the cotillion. "As I have guessed the source of your contentment, will you not tell me who it is?" Felix opened his mouth to say that no, he was not at all enamored of any particular young lady, only to recall the young woman from whom he had taken the brooch. He had been searching for her for over a sennight and had not discovered her as yet, which was, much to his chagrin, rather frustrating. This pause appeared to be more than enough for Lord Bramwell who immediately threw his head back, laughed aloud and then jabbed one finger into Felix's shoulder. "I knew it." His eyes sparkled and Felix groaned, closing his eyes, and rolling his head back. "You will not tell me, I see, but I am certain that I am correct."

I must find a way out of this conversation.

Pausing, Felix twisted his lips for a moment and then let out a long and heavy sigh.

"I will confess I *have* noted someone of late."

"Is it because of her beauty? Because of the way she entrances you?"

The mirth in Lord Bramwell's tone had Felix chuckling but he shook his head.

"No, you must understand me. There is a young woman I have considered of late, but it is not because she is fair of face, or of excellent character. Rather, it is because I find her so very forthright and therefore distinct from every other young lady."

"Oh." At this, Lord Bramwell's face fell, his smile disappearing. "So you think her different rather than of any particular beauty? That does not mean your heart has been taken, then."

Relief pooled in Felix's stomach.

"Certainly not! I consider her, not because I have any intentions of matrimony, nor even of courtship, but because she is very different from every young lady in London." Chortling, he put one hand on his friend's shoulder. "However, she is not of marriageable material... not even to a gentleman such as I!" This last part was not at all true, for he was quite certain that the young lady would be *more* than suitable for matrimony, had he the intention of chasing her, but he did not want Lord Bramwell's questions to continue. He was hiding a good deal from him already, so what would be a little more? "Have you thought to pursue any particular young lady yourself?" His eyebrows lifted in question as Lord Bramwell frowned. "After all, you were the one speaking of thinking of such things. Is there anyone who has captured your attention as yet? Shall I hear banns called very soon?"

"If there is, I shall not inform you." Lord Bramwell lifted his chin, his eyebrows low, eyes dark. "Mayhap I shall not even introduce any young lady I consider to you, given that you mock the very idea of matrimony!"

"I do not mock it," Felix answered, quickly. "It is not

something I am considering and if you seek to, then I swear to you, I shall not say a word against you."

Putting one hand to his heart, he grinned back at his friend, but Lord Bramwell only rolled his eyes. Inwardly triumphing over the fact that he had managed to keep the secret about his highwayman ways, as well as about the young lady, entirely to himself, Felix turned his attention back to the other guests in the ballroom.

What if she is here this evening?

It was a little frustrating to him that, several days later, he still had no idea of her name and title nor of who her father was, but a highwayman did not demand to know the name nor the title of the lady or gentleman they were stealing from. Why should such a fellow care? All the same, he had been a little irritated that he had not asked her, for she might well have offered him her title, had he asked for it.

"Mayhap I ought not to believe you." Lord Bramwell sniffed, glancing at Felix, but he barely heard his friend speak. "Mayhap you tease me to distract me from the truth! It would be very like you to do such a thing."

Felix did not answer. Instead, his attention was entirely taken up by a young lady who had, just now, walked into the room. He could hardly believe his luck. For the last several days, he had spent every day and night attending almost every soiree, afternoon tea, dinner, or ball he could manage, in the hope of seeing her again, but as yet he had been entirely unlucky. Quite why he had been driven to do such a thing, he could not say, but he had told himself that it was simply so that he could find a way to return the brooch.

And now, there she was.

The young lady was walking beside an older lady whom he recognized to be her mother. She was not deliberately coming towards them, of course, but Felix found himself smiling all the same. She appeared almost regal in her countenance, her head lifted, her shoulders back, and a graceful smile upon her lips. All in all, he found her quite breathtaking, just as he had found her on the day that he had stolen her brooch.

Lord Bramwell's voice faded into the distance as Felix set his eyes upon the young lady. She smiled, obviously acquainted with someone near her, and he found himself smiling back as though it was he that she was greeting. Now that he had come upon the lady again, he was finally going to be able to obtain an introduction to her, to learn her name and her situation. He would have to find a way to return the brooch to her, albeit without her knowledge, but that was not important for the moment. The only thing he desired was to make her acquaintance.

"Are you certain that there is no one who had gained your particular interest?" Lord Bramwell chuckled, nudging Felix lightly. "You suddenly appear utterly transfixed, and I begin to wonder if I have not been something of a fool to have believed what you told me!"

Quickly seeing just how unguarded he had been in his manner, Felix looked around for an excuse.

"I was thinking to myself about how ridiculous Lord Jennings looks this evening."

The answer came quickly and much to Felix's relief, it appeared to satisfy Lord Bramwell's questions, for he immediately looked for the fellow and then laughed aloud. Lord Jennings was nothing more than a fop, and for the moment, it was enough to distract Lord Bramwell from the truth.

"He is particularly garish this evening, I must admit!"

Lord Bramwell's interest passed, and Felix let out a slow

breath of relief as his friend continued speaking of Lord Jennings' attire. Felix still had every intention of achieving an introduction to the young lady at some point during the evening, but for the moment he held himself back. He had to be careful and cautious or risk his friend's gentle teasing for many days to come.

CHAPTER THREE

"It must have been quite a terror for you."

Elizabeth smiled rather blandly as Lady Derriford looked from her back to her mother.

"It was greatly distressing." Lady Longford sighed and pressed one hand to her forehead. "I am still quite overcome by the experience."

This was the fourth time that evening that her mother had spoken of the attack by the highwayman, and Elizabeth was becoming both weary of it and embarrassed by it. They had been a sennight in London so far, during which time her mother had taken to her bed and had refused to move from it. Given that Elizabeth had no one but her mother to chaperone her, she had been forced to linger in the house. Her attempts to encourage her mother from her bed had been futile and it was not until Lady Winthrop – one of her mother's dearest friends – had come to call that Elizabeth had felt the first flicker of hope.

Lady Winthrop had only just arrived in London but, having heard the dreadful story, had quickly made her way to the house. Whatever it was that she had said to Lady

Longford, it had encouraged her to rise from her bed - much to Elizabeth's relief! She had not been able to rejoice immediately, however, for there had been much discussion about whether or not Lady Longford was quite prepared, if she had enough strength of both mind and body, to return to society.

Elizabeth had said nothing, knowing that her words would have little effect on her mother. It took many hours but, eventually, Lady Longford had decided that, yes, she *would* be able to step back into society and thus, plans to attend this evening's ball had been made. Lady Longford had stated various things, such as the fact that she certainly would not be able to stand for too long, but Elizabeth had made her various assurances and thus, they were now standing – or sitting - in the midst of a London ball. Elizabeth delighted in the sounds of conversation, in the colors and the music all swirling around her, and finally allowed herself to smile.

"Lady Yardley!"

Hearing her mother's exclamation, Elizabeth turned around quickly only to be embraced by none other than Lady Yardley herself. Her heart lifted all the more as she saw that there were two of her friends present also, and she embraced each one in turn, a little surprised that tears burned in the corners of her eyes.

"It is truly so wonderful to see you all." Blinking quickly, she pushed the moisture away, knowing that she could not let a single tear fall when she was in company, for fear that her mother would then exclaim that she was overcome with weakness again and might urge her to return home. "I am so glad to be in London again."

"As we are glad to see you." Miss Millington smiled gently. "You did receive my note, I hope?"

"Yes, and I was glad for it." A letter had come from Miss Millington only two days before, stating that she was only a short distance from London, and was eagerly looking forward to seeing Elizabeth again. "I am glad that you and your family arrived safely."

"And they were not beset by highwaymen." Lady Yardley shook her head. "It must have been very distressing for you."

"Indeed it was." Elizabeth did not turn back to face her mother as she spoke, keeping her voice low. "My mother has also found it very distressing indeed."

This was said without any further explanation, but from the nod and the small smile on Lady Yardley's face, Elizabeth felt sure that she understood.

"Lady Yardley, I was hoping that I might speak with you." Lady Longford waved weakly in Lady Yardley's direction, having chosen to sit rather than stand. "As you know, we were set upon in the most dreadful fashion as we made our way to London. I have still not quite recovered from the shock and thus, I fear, I will not be able to take my daughter into London society as I had hoped."

Elizabeth blinked. This was the first that she had heard of her mother speaking so, fearing that she now intended to return to her bed. Or was it that she simply wished to linger in this state of supposed weakness, to garner a little more sympathy from the *ton*?

Lady Yardley did not hesitate.

"Permit me then to step in where you cannot," she said, quickly. "I should be very glad to offer my aid to Lady Elizabeth, if you would be satisfied with that?"

"I would be so very grateful." Pulling out her fan, Lady Longford waved it vaguely in front of her face. "I do not think myself capable of the task."

"Then allow me to begin by taking Lady Elizabeth for a short turn around the ballroom." Lady Yardley smiled widely and then turned to Elizabeth, a question in her eyes. With a nod and a smile to her mother, Elizabeth followed Lady Yardley quickly, along with the rest of her friends, uncertain whether to feel embarrassed or relieved at the strange situation which she now found herself. To her mind, her mother was more than capable, but clearly, Lady Longford had decided otherwise. Her mother had, on occasion in the past, taken to her bed over some trifle, but it had never been for long. It seemed now that she was to do the same here. "I take it that the last sennight has been a little... trying?"

Thinking that it was best to hide nothing from Lady Yardley, Elizabeth sighed.

"Yes, it has been very difficult. My mother has insisted that she remain in her bed and, despite my encouragement, would not move from it. I feared that we might have to return home and, truthfully, Lady Yardley, I had no expectation of her asking such a thing of you. I do hope that you do not mind becoming my chaperone, even though my mother is more than capable of filling that role, in my opinion."

Lady Yardley smiled sympathetically but then touched Elizabeth's arm for a moment.

"Do be gentle to your mother," she advised quietly. "A highwayman is no laughing matter, and the shock of being set upon in such a way must have been very great indeed. She may find herself truly upset by it, to the point that she does not feel that she is able to do as she ought, for you. Her concern is touching, is it not?"

Elizabeth hesitated before she replied, considering all

that Lady Yardley had said, and finding herself with a sense of being a little admonished - justifiably so, perhaps.

"Mayhap I have been a little harsh in my frustrations." She smiled ruefully as Lady Yardley looked back at her. "I will do as you suggest. I am very grateful to you. I do not think I would be able to traverse society without your help, for I would otherwise have to cling to my mother!"

"And I am truly contented to assist you. I am certain that, this Season, we shall find both yourself and Miss Millington very happily settled."

Elizabeth lifted her shoulders gently and then let them fall.

"I am still quite determined. I will not settle for a gentleman who does not care for me, and for whom I care very little in return."

Lady Yardley nodded and smiled, and her response was something of a gentle relief to Elizabeth, who thus far had found herself battling against Lady Longford's response to her desire.

"That is just as it should be, and I do admire you for that." Gesturing to the room in front of them, Lady Yardley chuckled. "However, I am sure that in amongst all of these very fine fellows, there will be someone who is more than half in love with you already – or who will be quite ready to fall in love with you the moment you meet."

Elizabeth, liking the idea but thinking it a little implausible, found herself laughing.

"That would be a very fine thing indeed, Lady Yardley," she admitted. "Ah, how good it is to be back in company again."

"It certainly is."

A gentleman Elizabeth did not recognize responded to

Elizabeth's remark, smiling first at Lady Yardley, and then to her.

"Forgive me for the interruption." Inclining his head, he looked at Lady Yardley. "Good evening, Lady Yardley. I see that you have returned to London for this Season. Is your husband here with you?"

Lady Yardley smiled.

"He intends to join me very soon. There are a few affairs at the estate which require his attention."

"A most responsible fellow, as he always has been."

The gentleman shot an inquiring glance towards Elizabeth as he spoke. She took him in, looking back at him and seeing his amiable smile and his eyes which swept down her form and then rose to her face again. Her skin burned, and a flush rose to her cheeks. Most gentlemen were not as unguarded as this fellow, although she could not distinguish whether her response came from anger or mortification at being looked at in such a way.

"Allow me to make the introductions." Lady Yardley tilted her head towards Lady Elizabeth. "This is Lady Elizabeth, daughter to the Earl of Longford. And this," she continued, gesturing to the gentleman, "this is Viscount Winterbrook."

She dropped into a curtsey.

"I am very glad to make your acquaintance."

"As I am to make yours." He dropped into a low bow, then smiled back at her. "You must forgive me for interrupting your conversation with Lady Yardley. It is only that I am acquainted with her husband, and wondered if he too was in London for the Season. Permit me to step back and allow you to continue."

"There is no need to do so."

Elizabeth spoke quickly, finding that Lord Winterbrook

was a very handsome gentleman, and that she was eager for his company. He had an easy smile, which always seemed to be present, regardless of what they were speaking of, and green eyes which flashed from place to place without hesitation. He did not seem to care that she had noticed him watching her and was, she considered, rather bold in his manner. Elizabeth was not certain if that was something she liked.

"And are you dancing this evening?" A hopeful eagerness lifted his voice a little. "It would be very uncouth of me to be introduced to such a beautiful young lady and then choose not to request her dance card."

The way that his eyes danced about as he smiled at her sent a gentle, curling sensation into the pit of her stomach. Elizabeth could not explain it, for it was the most unusual sensation, and one she had not experienced before, but yet, it was not entirely unwelcome.

"I am to dance this evening, yes." She offered him a small smile. "I am afraid that I have only just arrived and therefore my dance card is entirely empty."

"I do not think that a bad thing in the least!" Lord Winterbrook exclaimed. "Rather, I find it quite delightful, for it means that I will have the choice of dances from you this evening." Elizabeth smiled and handed him her dance card, looking at Lady Yardley, who was, for some unknown reason, smiling very broadly indeed. Recalling what she had said about a gentleman falling instantly in love with her upon introduction, Elizabeth's cheeks warmed. Surely Lady Yardley could not think that Lord Winterbrook would be such a fellow! "Have you permission to waltz, Lady Elizabeth?" Lord Winterbrook lifted his head, his pencil poised over the card. "I should not like to sign my name there if you are not permitted to do so."

For some entirely confusing reason, Elizabeth's cheeks grew hot.

"Yes, I have been given permission to waltz, Lord Winterbrook." It was a question which she had been asked before, so why she should become hot and flustered when Lord Winterbrook had asked her the question she could not quite understand.

"Wonderful!" Lord Winterbrook wrote his initials, then handed the dance card to her. "I look forward to our dance, Lady Elizabeth." With a smile, he inclined his head towards her, and then to Lady Yardley. "And now I shall leave you. Excuse me."

Her eyes fastened themselves to him as Lord Winterbrook walked away. She could not understand why his presence had made her feel so unaccountably odd but all the same, she could not pretend that she felt nothing.

"You see?" Lady Yardley laughed, her arm through Elizabeth's. "You shall have every gentleman in London falling at your feet this Season, I am sure of it. Lord Winterbrook is just the beginning."

Elizabeth managed a smile.

"I hope that you are right, Lady Yardley," she answered, carefully. "And I hope that I will not make a fool of myself dancing the waltz! It has been some time since I stepped out for such a dance."

"I am certain that in Lord Winterbrook's arms, you will be more than contented," Lady Yardley said firmly. "You need not fear. This evening is the beginning of a wonderful Season for you."

CHAPTER FOUR

*E*xcitement sent a thrill through Felix's veins as he rode his horse faster and faster, chasing the carriage. One of the men who rode with him waved his pistol, coming alongside the driver, who had been going at a somewhat sedate pace.

"Stop!" Felix exclaimed, as his men surrounded the carriage. "You must stop at once!" He kept his eyes fixed on the coachman, for on occasion a coachman had himself been armed, but it appeared that on this occasion, the man was nothing of the sort. When the carriage came to a stop, the coachman held both hands up on either side of his face, the reins now languishing in his lap. "A very wise decision." Jumping down from his horse, he waited for the men to take their positions. One stood in front of the horses, still astride his own horse, with the other by the coachman's side, holding a pistol threateningly in the coachman's direction. The third man stood back, ready to assist in whatever way was required. "Now." Walking to the carriage, Felix tapped on the window, peering inside. "Open the door and come out - and if you do not, then I shall come in myself."

The door was eventually pushed open and without hesitation, Felix stepped to look inside. He was met by the white faces of the two people within. One was an elderly gentleman and the other a young lady. There must be a connection between them, he supposed, studying them in silence. Was she his daughter? He appeared a little too old to be her father but, then again, Felix considered, he might have been a gentleman who had married later in life and thereafter, fathered children much later on in his years.

"Good afternoon." He inclined his head. "I have come to unburden you from some of your wealth."

"Is that so?" The gentleman looked straight out at Felix. His dark eyes glinted in stark contrast to the whiteness of his face. "And what if we have no wealth?"

Laughing, Felix shook his head.

"A likely excuse," he grinned, "but one which has been offered to me on many an occasion already. I am afraid that I do not believe you."

"But it is the truth." The young woman blinked rapidly as tears formed in her eyes, but Felix was unmoved. He had already seen many young women fall into floods of tears at the thought of having some of her precious possessions taken from her. "We have so little."

"And from that supposed little," Felix stated. "I shall take *some*." Waving his pistol gently, he looked first at the lady, and then at the gentleman. "Do not think that I am afraid to use this if required." This was, of course, a complete lie, for there was no circumstance that would induce Felix to shoot anyone, particularly when they had done nothing wrong. "You must have some jewels, miss?"

The young woman's tears began to fall down her cheeks.

"The only thing I have is my locket."

Finding it from around her neck, she took it out for him to see and, to Felix's surprise, it was a very simple, unadorned locket. No doubt it had some sort of sentimental value, although it was nothing overly expensive.

Felix shook his head.

"I do not believe that is all you possess. You must have something more, perhaps in your luggage?"

"And what luggage is it you think we have?" The gentleman's eyes pierced his again. "Did you not see that as you approached our carriage? We have no luggage to speak of. Here I have only one bag for myself and one for my niece."

"Your niece?"

The man nodded.

"Yes, this is my niece, Miss Whitford. I am Mr. Harrison, her granduncle. I promise you that we have no wealth. I have used near all of it to take Miss Whitford to London in an attempt to find her a suitable match... before the *ton* hears of her circumstances."

Felix frowned. There was truth in the man's expression and the prick of conscience bit down at him hard.

"And what circumstances would these be?"

Doubts still rose in his mind, but as he looked at the young lady and saw her tears, his heart constricted. Realizing that Harrison had spoken the truth about their luggage, his concern began to grow.

"I shall explain, uncle." Miss Whitford dabbed at her eyes with the edge of her sleeve before sniffing lightly, then looking at him. Her voice was soft, her face pale but her words held truth. "My mother was fortunate enough to marry a gentleman of wealth, even though her standing was not akin to his own. I believe they loved each other dearly. However, he'd already had a son with his late wife. A son who is now Lord Ruthven, due to my father no longer being of this earth." The young woman blinked rapidly but her voice was steady. "I was born a year or so after my parents' marriage, but I barely knew my stepbrother, since he was sent to Eton when I was young. Sadly, my mother passed away a little over a year ago and I have been mourning her ever since." A slight wobble in her voice indicated the depths of her emotion. "A little over a fortnight ago, I was informed that I was to leave the house at once. I was forced to bid farewell to the house I grew up in, the only place I have ever called home. With nowhere else to go, I went to my uncle and he, in turn, suggested that we go to London." Her eyes welled up with tears again. "My stepbrother forced me from the house, and I was allowed to take nothing with me, so we have no wealth to speak of. However, I am still the daughter of a gentleman and mayhap, I might have a chance to find a suitable match." Her eyes closed as tears dripped from her cheeks. "*Before* it becomes clear that my stepbrother has practically disowned me."

Instead of refusing to believe this story, Felix's first thoughts and feelings were ones of anger. He was acquainted with Lord Ruthven and could not understand why the man would treat his stepsister in such a way! A gentleman's responsibility was to his own family, and *he* ought to be the one taking care of his stepsister, making certain that she was provided for and found a suitable match. Clearly, instead of doing so, he had simply decided she was a burden he did not require, and therefore, had dismissed her without consideration.

"I do not have a great deal of coin myself." The older gentleman dropped his head, a slight flush at his throat. "But I have enough to take us to London and to, thereafter, secure us lodgings for a month or so." His head lifted a little. "I am a godly man. I pray frequently and now do so solely for my niece, with the fervent hope that the Almighty might see fit to answer my prayers."

"And where have you taken lodgings?" Felix found himself saying, even though he had no intention of speaking so. "Where is it that you will be staying?"

"I have found a place."

The gentleman took a moment to answer, perhaps a little surprised that a highwayman should be asking him such questions. When Felix lifted an eyebrow, he named the place, and Felix immediately shook his head. The place named was not suitable, not even for the gentleman, and certainly not for the young lady.

The story of the young lady's situation and the kindness of her granduncle's heart had brought about a feeling of sympathy in Felix. He had no intention of taking the lady's locket nor of demanding coin from the gentleman. Instead, he took a breath and shook his head.

"I cannot know for certain whether such a story is true, but I do find that my sympathies are engaged." Placing his pistol down on the floor of the carriage, he looked directly at the older gentleman. "But your niece cannot stay in those lodgings. I may be a highwayman, but even *I* know that such places are not suitable for young ladies."

The older gentleman's eyes glistened.

"This is all I can afford, sir." The slight wobble to his voice had Felix's heart twisting. "Do you not understand? All she has is that locket. Nothing more. It is just as well that she hid the locket under her dress as she removed herself from the house, for I am certain that Lord Ruthven would have taken it from her had he been aware of it. He was determined to leave her with nothing and therefore, I must give all that I have to give her even a chance of a happiness."

Felix's throat constricted. They had faced so much pain already, he could not allow them to go to London to face even more difficult circumstances! At the same time, however, he did not want to give himself away nor ruin his reputation as a highwayman. He had always enjoyed what he did as regarded putting on the mask and chasing after various carriages – but that thrill of excitement was no longer with him. His heart sank as he looked into the face of the young woman and saw the paleness of her features, the tears in her eyes. Was her fear really something he found delight in?

Felix shuddered, then turned his face away.

"I know many gentlemen and ladies in London." Speaking carefully so he would not reveal himself, he let out a heavy breath. "This will sound a little strange, but I will tell you now to make your way to Lord Winterbrook's townhouse. Tell him your situation. Express your concern to him. I am certain he will be able to help you."

The gentleman shook his head.

"I cannot simply turn up on the doorstep of someone I have never met, particularly when I am as lowly as this!"

"But you cannot take your niece to the East End of London." Felix spoke as gently and carefully as he could, not wanting to frighten the young lady, but needing to be honest, also. "It will be all the worse for her and for you, I am afraid. Is that what you wish for? Do you wish for yourself to be injured, thrown about, or beaten until you can barely move? Do you wish to see ruffians and scoundrels take everything – and anything - they wish... from you both?" Letting his eyes shift to the young lady for a moment, he returned his attention to the older gentleman and watched as the color drained from his face. The young woman's eyes had gone very wide indeed, and for a moment, he feared she might cast up her accounts, only for her eyes to close as she shuddered violently. "If you will not go to Lord Winterbrook, then you might go to Lord Bramwell." Felix shrugged. "Both are gentlemen of generosity, and both I know are acquainted with Lord Ruthven. They *will* help you."

The young woman spoke, her voice quavering.

"This is most peculiar. Why ever should you be advising us as such? Would it not be best to simply snatch my locket and ride away?"

Felix smiled and stepped back from the carriage door.

"Mayhap I should, but do not believe that all highwaymen are as wicked as they appear. I have sworn never to take from those who cannot afford it, and I believe your story." Sweeping into a great bow, he stepped back with a flourish. "And now, to prove my words to you, I shall leave you to continue on your way. I must hope that you will do as I have instructed, sir." He fixed his gaze on the older gentleman, who gave an almost imperceptible nod. "Make your way to one of these two gentlemen rather than to lodgings in the East End. There is no shame in asking for aid." With a lift of his chin, he gestured to his men to step back. "Goodbye."

He pushed the carriage door shut and, with a wave of his hand, encouraged the coachman to pick up the reins and move away without any further incident.

"What exactly are you doing?"

Felix turned to see his other three companions all looking at him, with the first ripping the mask from his face to reveal a heavyset frown and eyes that sparked with anger.

"I have decided not to take anything from these two." Felix shrugged. "But of course, since I pay you for riding with me – pay you handsomely, I might add, I do not think that you can have any complaint."

One of the other men came a little closer, still astride his horse which was, Felix had to admit, a little intimidating. Mounting quickly so he would be at the same height as the men, he held the second man's gaze steadily. The three men he had hired were all equally roguish, but he had considered, given he would pay them well, that he need not fear them. He had enough wealth to do so, which meant it would matter very little to them what he did with what he stole. Or indeed, if he chose not to steal anything from anyone at all!

"You're still going to pay us for this ride?"

Whether it was a question or a statement, Felix was not sure, but he nodded firmly.

"I will pay you regardless of what takes place on any ride we take together," he said firmly. "You do not seem to understand, so allow me to make myself quite clear. I will pay you every time, regardless of what I take or what I do not take. Therefore, whether I decide to steal from a gentleman or I choose to step back, you will be given the same amount as has been promised. Do I make myself quite clear?" The three men glanced at each other, with the other two removing their masks also. Eventually, one of them nodded. "Of course, if you wish to leave my employ, you may do so. That is your choice." Shrugging, he gestured towards London. "I am very sure that I will be able to find someone to replace you quite easily. After all, consider your companions and friends who would be looking for such a situation as this! Please, if you have anyone you think would be suitable to fill your position, then do send them to me."

One of the men muttered something, but he then shook his head when Felix lifted an eyebrow in his direction.

Obviously, the man had no intention of answering, and thus, with a shrug, Felix wheeled his horse around and turned its nose back towards London. Whether or not he would be able to get ahead of the carriage, he was not sure but, even if he could not do so, he knew his butler would encourage the gentleman and the young lady to remain until he arrived home. Quite what to do with him was not yet clear but, initially, he would have to play pretense, horrified that a highwayman had recommended him and questioning who such a person may be! However, when it came to it, Felix was eager to aid Miss Whitford and her uncle after they had been treated so cruelly by Lord Ruthven. To have thrown his stepsister aside was utterly despicable in Felix's eyes, and regardless of the fact he sometimes pretended to be a highwayman and stole things from other members of society, Felix was quite determined to step forth in goodness and extend a hand of generosity to these poor folk.

A sudden thought crossed his mind and he smiled, his whole body suddenly alive with both mirth and eagerness.

Lord Bramwell has been considering matrimony. The smile spread into a grin, and he chuckled aloud, then leaned forward over his saddle, urging his horse a little faster. This afternoon had gone in an unexpected direction, but mayhap, in the end, it had done him some good.

CHAPTER FIVE

"This may sound a little ridiculous, but I did wonder if we might use the Ledger to discover the true faces of the highwayman."

Lady Yardley, Miss Millington, and Lady Sherbourne listened carefully as Elizabeth recounted what had happened to her – albeit without the kiss.

"I am very grateful to you, Lady Yardley, for stepping into my mother's place, but I am also aware that the situation affects not only myself and my mother. Surely these men will be attacking other persons and other carriages! Is there a way for them to be stopped?"

"It is a particular problem, especially for those coming into London," Lady Yardley murmured. "It is not very easy to find out the true identity of such people. What makes you think that this highwayman is different?"

Elizabeth bit her lip, suddenly uncertain.

"The truth is, I found this highwayman a little... unusual," she answered, pushing away the warmth which began to pulse through her veins when she thought of him. "He seemed more eager to talk than to force me to hand over my jewels. It was most unexpected, I confess! He even offered to allow both myself and my mother to remove ourselves from the situation without injury, provided I spoke at length with him first." Upon seeing Lady Yardley's eyebrows lift high, she nodded and let out a dry laugh. "That is precisely my feeling. Why would a highwayman do such a thing as that? It was as if he did not have any need for the brooch I provided him, as though he were only doing it out of the desire to behave in a reckless manner." Another thought came to her, and her eyes widened. "Indeed, now that I think of it, his speech was very unusual also. He spoke as any gentleman of the *ton* might do, not in a rougher tone, as I might have expected."

Lady Yardley blinked.

"You mean to say -?"

"You think that the highwayman is a gentleman in society!"

Miss Millington's exclamation came just as Lady Yardley said almost the same thing. Elizabeth hesitated, then put out both hands, a little unsure.

"I cannot say for certain, but my instinct would be to suggest that he is certainly from a higher standing than those we might first consider when thinking of a highwayman." Her lips pressed tightly together. "Do you think that the Ledger might be able to help in some way?"

Lady Yardley hesitated for a moment.

"Mayhap. We might put in a notice enquiring as to whether or not anyone else has been set upon by this highwayman? We could put in a brief description of him and see if there are any stories that we can use. There might be clues by which we could begin to decipher his identity." She lifted both shoulders. "That is all I can suggest for the moment."

Elizabeth let out a breath and with it came a smile.

"That is certainly something. I hope that you do not think me foolish to be thinking on this so."

"Not in the least!" Lady Yardley exclaimed, as the others shook their heads. "You wish to identify him to aid society. That is an excellent idea."

Elizabeth smiled softly.

"Thank you." Her smile twisted. "Though quite what I am to do when I *do* discover him is a little uncertain!"

"You could demand the return of your brooch, at the very least!" Lady Sherbourne suggested, smiling briefly. "I am sorry that he took that from you."

"Thank you."

She dropped her gaze and clasped her hands gently in her lap, aware of the heat behind her eyes. The heirloom had meant a great deal to her, for it was the only thing of her grandmother's which had been given to her. The thought of never having it again was a difficult thought.

"It is something we can try at least." Lady Yardley smiled, then changed the subject. "Now are you to attend the ball this evening? Have you any gentleman in your thoughts at present?" She looked at Elizabeth first and then at Miss Millington. "I know there have been many gentlemen seeking you out!"

Elizabeth, glad to be speaking on another topic, shook her head.

"I confess that I have been quite taken up with either thinking about the highwayman, my missing brooch, or my dear Mama." She offered Lady Yardley a brief smile. "Mama *has* appeared quite fatigued of late. I cannot tell the reason behind it, and I have suggested the physician, but she states now that further rest is what will aid her. I am grateful for your willingness to chaperone me, for I do not think that she will be able to attend many events for some time yet."

Lady Yardley's advice to be gentle in Elizabeth's consideration of her mother had been quite correct for, in doing so and pushing her exasperation away, Elizabeth had seen just how tired her mother had become and how much strength the shock of the highwayman's actions had taken from her.

"But of course." Lady Yardley smiled again, then looked at Miss Millington.

"I am certain that both of you will find husbands by the end of the Season, as I have already said. I am sure this evening will be an excellent one."

"I hope it will be."

Elizabeth let her gaze fall to her lap, praying that this evening's festivities would take her mind off the highwayman entirely. She could only hope that the article in the Ledger would bring forth new names and fresh information about the fellow. What would it be like to look into his eyes again? To see the face of the man who had not only captured her brooch but also captured her lips?

Awash with heat, Elizabeth closed her eyes and swallowed tightly, deaf to the conversation around her.

Is it because I want to recover the brooch that I am so desperate to find him? Or is it because I cannot stop thinking about that kiss?

∽

"Look! I do believe Lord Winterbrook is approaching us!"

Nervousness tied a knot in Elizabeth's stomach as her eyes sought those of Lord Winterbrook. Again, he had that easy smile upon his face which always seemed so quick to appear and continually sent the strangest of sensations through her. She was still uncertain whether or not she liked this particular gentleman. His manner was much too easy, his boldness apparent. However, there was something about how he smiled at her that sent a surge of energy through her. If he was approaching to ask her to dance, it would be impossible for her to say no. Their last dances together had been quite wonderful, although the waltz had been a good deal more delightful than the other!

Lord Winterbrook was an excellent dancer, and it had been just as Lady Yardley had said: he had taken her into his arms, and she had quite forgotten her worries regarding her dance steps. She had done them all without hesitation, had found herself flowing freely with the music, sure of every step. All the same, her nervousness had remained. Something about being so close to Lord Winterbrook, something about looking into his eyes and seeing his smile directed solely at her, had been unsettling and wonderful in equal measure. All of this was why she was now uncertain as to whether or not she was glad to see Lord Winterbrook or desirous to push him away.

"He has danced with you before this evening, has he not?"

Miss Millington nudged her, speaking out of the corner of her mouth as Lord Winterbrook paused for a moment to greet another fellow.

"Yes, we have danced already on two occasions," she murmured, giving nothing more away.

It would be foolish to express how she was feeling for Lord Winterbrook, particularly when she had so much uncertainty herself.

At least I am not thinking of the highwayman.

A small smile touched her lips as he immediately came to mind, but she chased it away. How strange it was to think that she need not wonder what it would be like to be kissed any longer! Her first experience of a man doing so, boldly, was from a highwayman rather than a gentleman - which was, in itself, very unusual. She ought to be cross – furious even - that her first kiss had been stolen by a highwayman, someone so unworthy of such a thing – but try as she might, such an emotion would not rise within her. Much to her chagrin, there was almost a sense of gladness over it, for it had been both astonishing and enchanting in equal measure.

"Good evening. How pleasant to see you again." Lord Winterbrook smiled warmly, looking first at Elizabeth, and then looking to Miss Millington. "Miss Millington, good evening."

Curtseying, Miss Millington answered him warmly as Elizabeth looked on, studying him. He was a very charming fellow, certainly able to smile at almost anyone, and have them smile in return. Why was there a desire creeping up within her that his smile be directed solely at her alone?

"I did hear something about you, Lord Winterbrook," Miss Millington continued, making Elizabeth's eyebrows lift. "Though whether it be true or not, I cannot yet say."

Lord Winterbrook chuckled.

"Then pray, tell me what you have heard, Miss Millington, so that I might either disabuse you of it or confirm it is true." Wincing, he tipped his head a little. "I will confess that there are many things said about me, and not all of them are false."

She laughed and shook her head.

"This, I assure you, is a very good thing indeed." Glancing at Elizabeth, she smiled warmly. "It is said that you have taken into your house a young lady and her grandfather – people not particularly well known to you. Is that so?"

"Her grand*uncle*."

Elizabeth blinked in astonishment. Lord Winterbrook had taken someone into his house? Strangers to him? If it was a young lady, then had he intentions of marrying her? And if he did, then why did she suddenly feel a little ill at ease?

"Then it is true!" Miss Millington laughed. "Did I hear that they simply appeared at your house without expectation?"

Lord Winterbrook grinned but threw up both hands.

"It is most astonishing, certainly, but what was I to do but be charitable? It appears as though someone gave the elder gentleman my name, and told them that I would be willing to listen to him, and likely to express generosity. Given my supposed reputation – for I am not always as generous as was made out – it was not as though I could refuse!" Smiling, he dropped his hands. "There is one small correction. I have not taken them into my townhouse, but I have offered them another residence."

"Which you are paying for?" It was a most inappropriate question and Elizabeth's face burned when his eyebrows lifted, his gaze turning upon her. "Forgive me, I did not mean to pry."

"It is quite all right." Lord Winterbrook shrugged. "My mother has her own, smaller residence in London but given she is not in London at present, I have offered it to Miss Whitford and her granduncle."

"That is very generous of you."

He looked away as if he did not wish for her compliments.

"Their circumstances were so dark, I could not ignore

what had taken place. It appears that the young woman is stepsister to a gentleman known to me." Much to Elizabeth's surprise, a scowl darted across his face, chasing his smile away completely. She had never seen him with such a dark expression, and a slight chill ran down her spine, sending a gentle prickling to her skin. "I thought the gentleman was a good deal more... gentlemanly... than he is, it seems."

Hearing this account was slowly changing Elizabeth's opinion of Lord Winterbrook. Yes, he appeared to be rather bold, and certainly there was a tenacity about him that she could not deny, but it appeared that he had a most generous spirit and a deep sense of justice, wishing eagerly to do what he could to help those in such difficult circumstances.

And indeed it seems that he is very wealthy also.

The thought did not please her, for it was one of the reasons her mother had given to encourage her to entertain the suit of certain gentlemen. All the same, she considered, if Lord Winterbrook was ever to become more closely acquainted with her, then his wealth was something that might induce her mother to think well of him also.

"Might I ask what happened? Forgive me, I am not intentionally being bold, but I find the situation most astonishing."

"You think it strange that a gentleman would not care for his own stepsister?" Lord Winterbrook asked, his smile refusing to return. "In that regard, I would agree with you, Lady Elizabeth. Lord Ruthven is more selfish than I ever thought him. After the death of Lady Ruthven, his late father's wife, and Miss Whitford's mother - he told his stepsister to depart from the house, and that she was to take nothing with her." Tightening his jaw, he turned his head away. "His single act of kindness was to offer her the carriage to take her wherever she wished to go."

The darkness in his expression and his voice told her just how disagreeable he found the matter.

"Goodness." Elizabeth pressed one hand to her heart. "I cannot imagine her distress."

Lord Winterbrook sighed and looked back at her.

"She bore it with great strength and her granduncle has a more generous heart than I have ever seen. He was the only relative she could think of, the only one she had to depend on, and he offered her everything he had – even though he is a gentleman of low means. I believe that her mother married Lord Ruthven, having come from a lower situation than he. Miss Whitford's granduncle gave up almost everything he had to bring her to London. I have been glad to help both him and his niece. I have more than I require, and it pains me so to hear that a gentleman of my acquaintance would treat his stepsister in such a manner."

"Your kindness of heart is -" Elizabeth began, but Lord Winterbrook cut her off with a swift shake of his head.

"I say none of this to gain praise for myself." From the severity of his voice and the firmness of his gaze, Elizabeth believed every word. "I see the injustice in this, and it troubles me greatly. Should Lord Ruthven appear in London for the Season, I have every intention of making such feelings known."

An idea struck her, and Elizabeth took a small step closer to him.

"I might also have a suggestion. As you may know, Lady Yardley writes 'The London Ledger'. She is always careful about what is placed within it – any rumors or the like must be stated as such and she will only place them within her publication if they are to be of use to particular persons. In this case, would it not be good for society to hear about Lord Ruthven's treatment of his stepsister?"

Lord Winterbrook did not answer immediately. His eyes held hers, considering. His mouth tugged sharply to one side, but then, much to her relief, he nodded.

"That is a wise consideration, I must say." His smile had returned but held only a little warmth. "It pains me to have to even consider such a thing, but after how he has treated his own kin, I think that such a thing would be wise. The man deserves some punishment for what he has done, even if it is only the friendlessness of the *ton*."

"I find that I agree with you in that," she answered as Miss Millington nodded. "Might I ask if Miss Whitford would be eager to make my acquaintance? I would be glad to know her."

Immediately Lord Winterbrook's face lit up, his green eyes shining, his broad smile sending light into the entirety of his features. Even his voice had lifted a little.

"Would you be so willing, Lady Elizabeth? The reason she has come to London is, of course, in the hope of seeking a match. That is the only way to secure herself a comfortable future, and I know that she would be very grateful indeed to make your acquaintance. To have the friendship of an Earl's daughter would certainly lift her up in the eyes of society."

"But of course." Elizabeth smiled warmly. "I should be very glad to do so. Is she nearby?"

Lord Winterbrook turned his head, then looked back at her.

"Yes. I shall take you to her if you would like?"

"I should be glad to make her acquaintance also, but Lord Colton has asked me to dance with him for this next dance." Miss Millington smiled. "But might you bring her to make my acquaintance thereafter? It sounds as though she has been through a great deal, and I should like to offer her my friendship also."

Lord Winterbrook clapped both hands together, his smile growing into a beaming grin.

"You are both *very* generous. She will be so very pleased."

"Then let us go at once."

Elizabeth glanced at Lady Yardley, who was only a few steps away. She did not want to move away without the lady knowing.

"I shall inform Lady Yardley," Miss Millington said, seeing her hesitation. "I am sure that she will join you soon. I advise you to stay in sight of her as best you can, however."

"But of course."

With this, Lord Winterbrook offered Elizabeth his arm and she took it quickly, keenly aware of how the touch of her hand on his arm sent spiraling heat through her. Keeping her chin lifted, she averted her eyes from him for fear he would see all the things she was trying to hide from him. As they walked together across the ballroom, Lord Winterbrook glanced at her, then smiled, but said nothing, and Elizabeth felt her own smile grow in return. This Lord Winterbrook appeared to be a very different gentleman from the one she had first considered. His generosity, his kindness of spirit, and the softness of his heart built an admiration for him within her, and she found herself silently thinking that a gentleman such as he was a very rare sort of fellow indeed.

And perhaps a rather easy gentleman to fall in love with.

"Are you to dance this evening?" Lord Winterbrook murmured.

"I am."

His face split with another smile.

"Then would you allow me to sign your dance card once I have made the introductions to Miss Whitford?" Warmth settled over her hand as his free hand rested upon hers for a moment. "I should not like this evening to go by without dancing with you again."

Elizabeth nodded, the words sticking fast in her throat, and finally sliding free only when he took his hand away.

"Yes, I thank you."

It seemed now that her own heart was doing some very unfamiliar things when it came to Lord Winterbrook. It was both unexpected and uncertain, but the more she considered it, the less confusing it became.

Could it be that I am falling in love with Lord Winterbrook?

CHAPTER SIX

*R*iding out into the countryside, Felix took in a long breath, but found his discontent growing rather than fading - which was very odd indeed. The last few weeks he had found a great deal of happiness in his highwayman ways. The thrill of the pursuit, the highwayman disguise, the concealing of his true identity in place of another – it had all been the antidote he had required for his melancholy. Now, however, none of it offered him the same lifting of his spirits. Even now, as he stood watching, hoping for an approaching carriage, his heart felt rather heavy.

"There!"

One of the three men he had hired – Griggs, as he was known – pointed to where a carriage was trundling down the road, albeit at a somewhat sedate pace. It gleamed in the sunshine, and to Felix's trained eye, he considered that it was most likely the private carriage of a high-ranking gentleman.

"A private drag, I'm sure of it."

"Yes, I think so." Felix agreed but did not make any

moves to chase after it. "Step back, Griggs. You too, Stafford. In fact, pull back under the trees."

The third man did not move.

"But why not?" His tight jaw set, his eyes narrowing at Felix. "This is a perfectly good carriage. There's going to be a lot of fancy stuff in there for sure."

"And all the same, I said no, Connelly."

Felix shrugged off the need for any further explanation for he paid these men to do as he asked and nothing more. With a grunt, Connelly moved his horse back and Felix remained where he was, watching for another carriage to approach. His mind was in turmoil, questioning why he had pulled back, and yet understanding that the desire to chase after wealth was gone from him.

Perhaps I can take on a different venture.

Within the hour, there came another carriage. This one did not gleam in the sun as the other one had done. Instead, as he studied it carefully, he saw that it was much slower than the previous, only being pulled by two horses instead of four and with no grandeur about the carriage itself. His spirits suddenly lifted, and he realized what it was he wished to do. It was quite extraordinary, of course, for such actions were not what highwaymen were known for, but after his experience with Miss Whitford and her granduncle, his desires, it seemed, had changed significantly.

"*This* one."

Gesturing to the approaching carriage, he jammed his heels into the horse's sides and rode for it, with the three men coming after him. Very soon they had the carriage stopped, and the coachman, having no pistol on him either, sitting helplessly with the reins loose in his hands.

"I just hope that we get some good bounty here."

Felix looked across at Stafford.

"Regardless of what I take, you know full well that you gain nothing from this, aside from what I pay you."

Speaking firmly, he narrowed his eyes a little, though it was probably not seen given how his eyes were mostly hidden behind his mask.

"Yes, yes." The man waved a hand. "Though we were just thinking that maybe one day, if you take a great deal from these rides, you might think about paying us a little more."

With a snort, Felix threw out one hand towards Stafford in dismissal, and, with a lift of his chin, walked towards the carriage door. It opened before he even had a chance to knock upon it, and to his astonishment, a pistol was pointed in his face.

"I've been warned about the likes of you." A gentleman of an age with Felix brandished the weapon. "And you'd best get yourself away from here before you meet your end." The man had a firm jaw, and his eyes glinted. "Although maybe I should just shoot you regardless and do all of society a great favor."

Felix blinked.

"I would advise you to remove your pistol, sir." With a shrug, he gestured behind him, still holding his own pistol in his hand. "You have one shot but I, I am afraid, have four. You may very well kill me, but are you truly willing to lose your own life, as well as the lives of your companions?" It was an idle threat, of course, for he had no intention of killing anyone, and certainly would not allow his men to do so either. It seemed to have an impact upon the gentleman, however, for after a moment he began to lower his pistol, albeit with a dark scowl and a grunt of frustration. "Very good."

Stepping forward nimbly, Felix snatched the pistol from the man's hand and then dropped it to the grass beside him.

"What is it that you want?" The man's eyes were spitting with anger, the words flung from his lips. "You come to steal from us, do you not?"

"I do believe that is what a highwayman does," Felix replied with a smile, allowing the whisper of fear over being threatened so to drift away. "I quite understand that you do not wish me to take what is yours, of course." Lowering his pistol just a little, he kept his hand ready, but dropped his shoulders and took a small step back. "Why do you not tell me a little bit about yourself and those within your carriage? What are your names?"

"What difference would such a thing make to the likes of you?"

Felix shrugged.

"I like to be indulged," he responded, without giving any true explanation for his interest. "I might reconsider my thought of stealing from you if you were to tell me the truth of your situation." The man shook his head, clearly disbelieving this. "You must." Felix glanced at the other two occupants of the carriage. "Else I shall simply demand all you possess and leave you with nothing."

"Then you give me no choice." With a roll of his eyes, the man looked away as he spoke, as if he could not bear to even glance at Felix. "I am Baron Hereford, and this is my wife and her sister. We go to London."

"To find your sister-in-law a husband, no doubt," Felix responded, only for the Baron to shake his head.

"We take her to the Physician." The man scowled, his chin lifted. "She has been most unwell since the loss of her husband. We have been unable to lift her spirits and thus, as we see her wasting away, we must try anything we can to improve her condition."

There came a quieter voice from behind the gentleman, one softer and with tears coursing through it.

"The country Physicians and apothecaries have done nothing. A Physician in London is our last hope."

A little uncertain whether or not he should believe this fellow – for the man might easily have been telling a tale to force Felix away from him – Felix gestured for him to move out of his way. Stepping forward, he looked into the carriage to see where the second voice had come from, only to see a gaunt young woman staring back at him. Her cheekbones were sharp, her eyes seeming a little too large for her pale white face. Another woman was sitting beside her, one who looked a good deal more robust and in much better health. She was grasping the hand of the other, and from the similarities in their features he could tell that they were sisters. This one was the one who had spoken, it seemed.

Felix's heart filled with gentle sympathy.

"It seems as though you are in particular difficulty." With a small nod to the ladies, he said nothing more but stepped back, seeing Lord Hereford glance down at the ground where his pistol now lay. With a chuckle, Felix went to stand beside it. "I should not like to give you an opportunity to take back your pistol," he remarked as Lord Hereford's eyebrows lowered, his jaw working furiously. "However, I can see that what you have told me about your sister-in-law is the truth. I do hope that you find some help for her in the city though the Physicians in London can cost a great deal."

The gentleman shrugged.

"Gentlemen, such as myself, will do whatever we must for our family."

Felix nodded slowly and tilted his head, appreciative of the man's firm sense of duty.

"I have spoken to many, and stopped a multitude of carriages," he began slowly, an idea coming into his mind. "There is a Physician by the name of Oswald whom I know of. He was stopped some time ago, but appeared to be a very capable Physician, for one of my men sustained an injury and he chose to assist, with a manner both capable and efficient. I advise you to search for the Physician Oswald. He will be able to care for your sister-in-law best."

A good deal of what he had said had not been the truth, of course, but what else could Felix do? The truth was, he had heard of the Physician Oswald's sterling reputation, knowing him to be one of the very best in all of London, and sought out by almost all those in the *ton*. He was unsure as to whether Baron Hereford had heard of the Physician but hoped now that he would seek him out.

"And you think that I should accept the word of a highwayman?" Lord Hereford scoffed openly. "You say such a thing to garner something from me, no doubt."

"No, indeed not." Shrugging, Felix stepped back. "I say such a thing to be of aid to your sister-in-law."

Lord Hereford blinked, some of the anger fading from his expression.

"Then what is it that you will demand from me now?"

Felix smiled.

"Nothing." Picking up the pistol, he set it back into the carriage, careful to place it on the seat opposite the gentleman rather than hand it back to him directly. "Go to London. I hope that you find what you require there."

Lord Hereford's mouth fell open, but Felix did not wait. Instead, he mounted his horse and, signaling to the men, turned his horse to ride away. A glance behind him told him that Lord Hereford was still sitting there, staring after him, and it was the clearly written astonishment in the man's wide eyes and mouth ajar that had Felix laugh aloud as he rode through the wind.

～

"How very pleasant to see you again, Lady Elizabeth."

The way his heart leaped presented Felix with something of a difficulty. Yes, he had made the young lady's acquaintance with the intention of returning her brooch in some way, but he was now becoming rather fond of her, which was most inconsiderate of his heart. There was no thought in his mind of revealing the truth of his highwayman ways to anyone, especially not to a young lady, not even if her blue eyes were particularly delightful, or her smile sent his heart into a flutter. He had never expected himself to feel anything but general contentment after being in any young lady's company, but when it came to Lady Elizabeth, Felix realized he was beginning to seek her out at various events, which was all the more concerning to him.

"How pleasant to see you also."

The timbre of her voice expressed nothing but genuine delight, and when he asked for her dance card, she gave it willingly and with great speed, as though she had been hopeful of him doing so. Writing his initials for the quadrille, he paused for a moment, considering the second dance.

I want very much to take her waltz.

It would be the second time he had waltzed with her and would, no doubt, be noticed by some – including Lord Bramwell. Hesitating, he bit his lip. If he did not take her waltz, then another gentleman would do so. Glancing around him, he saw three other gentlemen standing near, each looking at Lady Elizabeth and, immediately, he wrote his initials for her waltz also. It seemed his heart did not want anyone else to waltz with her.

"I thank you."

Handing back her dance card, he smiled when Lady Elizabeth's eyebrows lifted a little.

"You have taken my waltz again. I see." Lady Elizabeth tilted her head to one side, her eyelashes fluttering just a little. "That means that my previous waltz was not as poorly danced as I feared."

"My dear lady!" Felix threw up his hands. "It was not poorly danced at all. You do not mean to say that you think I am a mediocre dancer, I hope?"

"No, indeed not!" Lady Elizabeth laughed and reached out to touch his hand for a moment. It was only a brief touch but the intensity it brought was quite extraordinary. "I found our dance most delightful. I was a little nervous, I confess, for I had not danced the waltz in some time."

"Well, I would never have known." It took him a moment longer than he had wanted to respond, finding his heart a little faster than before, his mouth suddenly dry. "Mayhap, Lady Elizabeth, we might do more than dance the waltz on occasion."

Her eyes widened and instantly, Felix squeezed his closed.

"Forgive me, I did not mean to suggest..." Taking a breath, he attempted to find the composure he was always so used to, only for it to evade him. "Allow me to make myself plain." With a small smile, he tipped his head to his right and then to his left, letting his eyes slide to either side as he did so. "I can see that our conversation must soon come to a close, for there are a good many gentlemen hovering around us, clearly eager to make your acquaintance or to steal your dance card for themselves." The words were coming a little more easily now and Felix managed a smile, relieved when she returned it. "I confess that I am a little frustrated that our time together must be ended. Perhaps I might come to call upon you?" Lady Elizabeth opened her mouth, only for Felix to recall something. "Although, wait a moment," he continued quickly before she had a chance to respond. "We might take a walk through the park instead, for I imagine a lady with your beauty and such a gentle character will, no doubt, have many gentlemen coming to call upon her. Therefore, I would once again be presented with the very same problem."

Lady Elizabeth put one hand on his arm, and Felix stuttered to a stop, slowly becoming aware that he had spoken very quickly indeed and without pause. He did not often find himself overcome in such a way, did not often find himself stumbling through what he wished to express. Why was it then, that simply by looking at her, he found himself doing so?"

"Are you asking if you might walk with me in the park, Lord Winterbrook?"

He nodded, pressing his lips together for fear that he might say more, and that it would come out in a torrent as it had done before. The last thing Lady Elizabeth required from him was to be overwhelmed, even though he feared he had done so already.

"I see." With a gentle smile that sent light into her features, she tilted her head. "Then I should be very glad to do so. What day do you propose we go together?"

He released a deep breath as his shoulders dropped, tension fading from him.

"Shall we say tomorrow?" Biting his lip, he frowned suddenly. "Or the day after that – or even the day that follows!" When she laughed, Felix paused, closed his eyes, and groaned. "Forgive me, Lady Elizabeth. Again, I am making something of a fool of myself." Lifting his chin, he looked directly at her. "What I mean to say is, I should be glad to walk with you in the park at any time when you are available, be it this week or the next. I will be glad to wait."

"That is very generous of you." Lady Elizabeth's cheeks were a little pink. "Shall we say tomorrow?"

What Felix had *not* expected was for his heart to leap so furiously that he could not catch his breath. This was not how he was! He knew himself to be a gentleman always stable with his emotions, never allowing anything to overwhelm him, refusing to permit a tug of his heart to affect his behavior. So why was he struggling to find a simple response? Why was he failing to make his delight known to her? All he was doing was standing mute, looking at Lady Elizabeth and she, with her gently lifted eyebrow, looking back at him.

"Lord Winterbrook?"

Felix cleared his throat and looked away, his face growing hot.

"Forgive me, Lady Elizabeth." Thinking that it would probably be best to tell her the truth, he allowed himself a small laugh. "You find me a little lost for words, such is my gladness. I did not think that you would be so eager in your willingness to walk with me, and I am truly happy because of it."

There came a blush into her cheeks, but Felix took the opportunity to incline his head and turn away. Excusing himself from her company. Immediately, three other gentlemen came into his place, but Felix walked away quickly with his head held high. Keeping a broad smile across his face, he waited until he was a short distance from her before he allowed it to fade.

I have never before felt such strength of emotion as this.

What was it about Lady Elizabeth which was capturing him so? Why was his heart so tumultuous in its beating? Why were his hands sweating, his forehead damp? Why had he fought to speak, why had he been unable to find the words which had so easily come to him before?

"Ho!"

Looking to his left, he saw Lord Bramwell beckon to him, but with a nod, he turned his head in the opposite direction. He was not about to go to his friend, who had, no doubt, seen Felix's interactions with Lady Elizabeth, and would thereafter see him dance with her again. Given how he was feeling at present, Felix had no intention of talking about Lady Elizabeth in any way, particularly when he did not understand things for himself. Instead, finding his way to a quieter corner of the ballroom, he leaned back against the wall and forced his breathing to steady.

Never did I think I would find my heart so captivated.

He had never thought that he would be captured by a young lady. He had always assumed that when the time came to marry, he would simply find someone who was the most suitable and thereafter, take her as his bride. Throughout his years, he had never believed that emotion was an important part of such a thing, and it was now both confusing and a little conflicting for him to be forced to consider that his notions of courtship, and even matrimony might be entirely wrong. He had asked to walk with Lady

Elizabeth, and the excitement in his heart when she had agreed was more than he had ever thought he would feel.

Felix dropped his head.

I cannot be falling in love with Lady Elizabeth, surely?

His eyes closed as he recalled their kiss. He had done that as the highwayman, and yes, it had only been an impulse but perhaps, somehow, it had bound his heart to hers. She was not the first young lady he had kissed, of course, but she was the first young lady who had roused any feelings within him.

With a sigh, Felix leaned his head back against the wall and closed his eyes. There would have to be a way to return the brooch to Lady Elizabeth without her knowledge, and, if he truly was to spend more time with her, to consider courting her, then he would have to consider abandoning his highwayman ways. If he wished to pursue it a little longer, he feared what would happen if Lady Elizabeth ever found out.

He would have to be very careful, if he was to be a gentleman in London *and* a highwayman and he would have to take great care that his worlds could never collide.

CHAPTER SEVEN

"You say a highwayman directed you to Lord Winterbrook?"

Astonishment widened her eyes, and she could barely take in what was being said to her by Miss Whitford. The young woman nodded so fervently that Elizabeth felt she had no choice but to believe her.

"I know it is most extraordinary, but it is the truth." Miss Whitford shook her head, seemingly still surprised at what had taken place. "My uncle – he is my granduncle, of course, but I do refer to him as my uncle - was to take us to lodgings somewhere in the East End of London. The highwayman, upon hearing this, appeared most unhappy with my uncle's decision. I did not think such a person would ever have any sympathy or regard for those he stopped, but in this case, it appears that he did. From what I recall, he practically made my uncle promise not to take me to the place he had originally intended us to stay."

"Most extraordinary indeed, as you have said." Elizabeth could not account for it, and she frowned a little as the two ladies walked arm in arm through Hyde Park. Lord

Winterbrook walked a little behind them in company with Mr. Harrison, and Elizabeth's mother was nearby also, although walking alone. Elizabeth smiled to herself. She was enjoying this afternoon immensely, albeit with a great deal of surprise surrounding their discussions about the highwayman. "Lord Winterbrook and your granduncle appear to be deep in conversation." Elizabeth murmured, as Miss Whitford glanced over her shoulder also. "It is good that they can talk so."

She and Lord Winterbrook had met, just at the entrance of Hyde Park, having intended to take their walk. They had not even begun to walk together, however, before Miss Whitford and her granduncle had appeared also, and greetings had been exchanged. It had seemed rude not to engage herself with the young lady and thus, Elizabeth's time with Lord Winterbrook was being a little interrupted. She could not blame the young woman, however, for it was clear that Miss Whitford needed a friend, and she was glad to be that to her.

Miss Whitford giggled as Elizabeth cast another glance at Lord Winterbrook over her shoulder.

"Have no fear, I shall free you to walk with him again soon."

Elizabeth blushed furiously and tried to laugh.

"It is no trouble, please. I am enjoying our walk."

"And yet, I am aware that you are *meant* to be walking with him. I shall leave you soon enough." Miss Whitford took a breath. "I think him a very kind gentleman, I must say."

"It appears that he is." Elizabeth smiled quietly, her heart quickening just a little at the thought of him. "I do not know Lord Winterbrook particularly well as yet, I confess. Indeed, I first thought him rather bold in his manner, and mayhap a little arrogant. But now I see that there is another aspect to his character also."

Miss Whitford looked at her for a moment, her gaze steady.

"You thought him arrogant?"

There was a hint of surprise there, but Elizabeth did not repond badly to it.

"Mayhap it is only because he seems so very sure of himself," she answered with a smile. "As I have said, I do not know him particularly well as yet."

"Which is why you are out taking a walk together, I suppose." Miss Whitford laughed softly. "I shall tell you something, but you must make certain that you do not let him know that I have told you, for he demanded that both I and my uncle keep it a secret."

For whatever reason, Elizabeth's heart bounced in her chest at these words, although she hesitated before responding.

"If Lord Winterbrook has asked you to keep something a secret, then I do not think you need to tell me."

Miss Whitford laughed.

"It is nothing of any seriousness. The only reason for such a request was to keep his generosity hidden from others," she shrugged and smiled again, "but I have no desire to keep it a secret, particularly if it means your opinion of him is a little improved."

Elizabeth, a little relieved, smiled.

"Very well."

Leaning a little closer to her, Miss Whitford's eyes danced.

"He has not only secured us lodgings – of which we are to bear no expense – but he has also given my uncle a great deal of coin, so that I might have new gowns and the like.

He has reimbursed my uncle for every penny he spent on taking me to London and indeed, offered him more for himself also. My uncle, I think, is a little unwilling to take it, given that he feels as though it may be charity. But I hope that he will do so. He has so very little and lives carefully with what he has." Her smile dropped. "It is not an easy life."

The thrill her heart sent through her was so enlivening, Elizabeth had to gasp. Was Lord Winterbrook truly so generous? Just how much of his character did he truly hide?

"That must be very trying for your uncle," she managed to say, still somewhat overcome by how generous Lord Winterbrook was being to two complete strangers. "And you say that he has no connection to you whatsoever?"

"None." Miss Whitford shook her head. "The only thing I know is that he is acquainted with my stepbrother, Lord Ruthven. I do not think he was particularly pleased to hear of my stepbrother's actions. Indeed, I confess he appeared rather angry. I felt right then that he was a gentleman of good character."

"If you are speaking of your stepbrother, Miss Whitford, let me disagree with you and state that, to my mind, he certainly does *not* have a good character." Lord Winterbrook came to join them, his deep voice sending a jolt of happiness through Elizabeth's heart. "Forgive me for the interruption, but your uncle wishes to return home. I believe he is a little fatigued."

"But of course." A note of concern entered Miss Whitford's voice as she stopped, turning to face Elizabeth while her eyes went to her uncle. "Thank you, Lord Winterbrook." Curtseying to Elizabeth, she smiled warmly. "I hope to see you again soon."

"Come to take tea with me tomorrow afternoon, if you

can. I will introduce you to some of my friends and Lady Yardley. She is the one who writes 'The London Ledger' and is most highly regarded."

Miss Whitford's eyes rounded, clearly all too aware of 'The London Ledger', making Elizabeth consider that mayhap, Lord Winterbrook had informed her about what was to be placed within it as regarded her stepbrother.

"That is very kind of you, Lady Elizabeth. I should like that very much."

"Then I shall send you a note with the details, later today."

Miss Whitford dropped into a curtsey again.

"Thank you. I look forward to it."

With a smile, Elizabeth watched as the young lady walked away, before allowing her gaze to drift to Lord Winterbrook. He too was looking after Miss Whitford and, much to her surprise, Elizabeth's jealousy began to burn. Frowning, she blew it out to embers, forcing her gaze elsewhere.

"That young lady has been very poorly treated indeed." With a scowl, Lord Winterbrook shook his head. "A most displeasing situation, I think."

"The situation where I hear you have been more than generous." Catching Lord Winterbrook's sharp look, she shrugged. "Miss Whitford was eager to inform me of your good character."

"Which she has no need to do," came the quick reply. "I am sure that it is just as any gentleman would do."

"And I am certain that it is *not*." When he offered his arm, Elizabeth took it without hesitation. "I do not think any gentleman needs to be generous to strangers, but yet you have decided to be so."

"I am acquainted with Lord Ruthven."

The tightness of his jaw stated precisely what it was he felt about the gentleman and Elizabeth let out a small sigh.

"He will receive a little comeuppance, I think. The Ledger will be printed this afternoon from what I understand, and it *will* contain an article about Lord Ruthven and what he has done... as well as a little about the highwaymen who have taken on so many carriages of late."

Lord Winterbrook started in evident surprise, twisting his head so quickly that she thought he might have pained it.

"The highwaymen?"

She nodded.

"Yes, that is so. It must have been something of a shock to hear that a highwayman was the one who told Miss Whitford and her uncle to go to you."

Lord Winterbrook cleared his throat, his eyes a little narrowed of focus.

"Oh. Yes, of course." He turned his eyes away again. "Yes, I suppose it was. However, I am glad that he did. After hearing the stories Miss Whitford has told me, I am greatly disturbed by her stepbrother's treatment of her. I do hope that she can make an appropriate match, so long as it can be encouraged."

Elizabeth, who had been about to ask whether Lord Winterbrook had ever thought about which of his acquaintances might be pretending to be a highwayman, now became fixed upon his last statement.

"I beg your pardon?"

"Forgive me." Another grin made his eyes twinkle as he looked at her. "It is only that I have a particular notion as regards Miss Whitford."

Rather than smile back at him, a lump formed in her throat, and she looked away, a little uncertain as to what it was that he was considering. Was it that he had plans to tie himself to Miss Whitford? She could not blame him for it, for, if that was his intention, then she was sure that Miss Whitford would make an excellent wife.

"You will not ask me what I mean?" Lord Winterbrook chuckled. "I see that you are quite determined to remain silent and behave as properly as you ought. Therefore, since you will not ask, I will tell you if you wish."

"Is it that you intend to find a suitable match for Miss Whitford?" Surprised that her voice was a little shrill, she coughed quietly. "Or do you plan to wed her yourself?"

It was a bold question, but she did not regret speaking it. The relief which came when Lord Winterbrook looked at her and then laughed made her smile brightly. Clearly, her thoughts had been quite mistaken.

"No, indeed, I have no intention of marrying her myself." Lord Winterbrook reached across and patted her hand on his arm. "I have no intention of being *that* generous, I confess! I will not give my heart away so freely. However, I know that one of my close friends is considering matrimony, and given that he is an amiable gentleman, and Miss Whitford an amiable young lady, I had wondered if the two of them might be aligned."

"I see." With a great swell of relief rising in her chest, Elizabeth smiled back at him, seeing the light in his eyes, and finding herself laughing softly. "You have plans to matchmake then, my Lord?"

"It seems as though I do." Lord Winterbrook answered but immediately winced. "I fear, however, that I may not be much good at it. If this does not work, then I shall be entirely unsure as to which gentlemen to introduce her to! Some might dismiss her without so much as a brief consideration and I do not want her to be injured."

How very kind he is.

"I can aid you in your plans." Elizabeth smiled softly when he looked at her. "Perhaps you do not need my aid but if I can encourage her in the direction of whichever friend this is, then I will be glad to do so." She squeezed his arm lightly. "Provided he is a gentleman of good standing, of course."

"He is certainly not a scoundrel!" Lord Winterbrook exclaimed with a broad smile. "It is my dear friend, Lord Bramwell. I think that he would be more than suitable for Miss Whitford and, if you would be willing to help me in this matter, I would be very appreciative."

Her heart lifted and she moved just a fraction closer, their steps slowing as they continued their walk through the park.

"I would be happy to," she answered firmly. "It will not be particularly difficult to speak well of Lord Bramwell, for I am acquainted with him. I assume that you also will encourage Lord Bramwell to consider Miss Whitford?"

"Certainly, I shall." Lord Winterbrook smiled, only for it to fade a little as he looked at her again, tilting his head just a fraction. "But is there not a slight concern that you might then take attention away from your own situation?" Speaking a good deal more quietly now, he frowned. "I would not want you to focus all of your attentions on Miss Whitford, without allowing *yourself* some consideration. Is it not the case that most young ladies seek a match while they are in London?"

"And I am no exception," Elizabeth answered with honesty. "This is my third Season, but I confess I have made something of a promise to myself, something my friends and I have all shared together."

Lord Winterbrook said nothing, but simply looked at

her. Elizabeth's face warmed, and she was aware that she had spoken rather freely. It seemed that he waited for her to say more, and, wondering whether or not she ought to express the situation to him, she shrugged inwardly, and then decided to be nothing but truthful. After all, if they were to strike up a closer acquaintance than they had at present, it would be best for him to understand precisely what she was seeking.

"My friends and I have always promised that we should never marry gentlemen who did not truly love us." Speaking slowly and carefully, Elizabeth made certain that her words were chosen with great distinction. "And whom we did not come to care for also. My friends – all bar one besides myself – have thus far found themselves successful in love, and I hope that I will soon be as they are."

Lord Winterbrook remained quiet for some moments. The heat of the sun blazed onto them, and Elizabeth's cheeks grew hotter still. She turned her head to the left, looking out across the park rather than paying any attention toward Lord Winterbrook, a little embarrassed that he had said nothing, and wondering at his reaction.

"And what if you should not find such a gentleman?"

His quiet question had her looking back at him.

"Then I shall not wed," she declared firmly. "I am all too aware that it is meant to be the sole delight and cause of every young woman in London to be married, but I confess that I find the idea of marrying simply for the sake of a good match to be most disagreeable. A gentleman may claim to be kind and genteel, but upon marriage become the entire opposite, revealing his true self. No, I wish to marry a fellow who loves me and who makes such a love plain. That way I can go into our marriage secure in his affections, and he secure in mine."

"Your determination is extraordinary." Lord Winterbrook took a deep breath and then let it out again with a slowness that pulled his brows low and tightened his jaw. "I hope that you have success, Lady Elizabeth."

"I thank you."

Nothing more was said of this, for Lord Winterbrook then began to talk of something else – the upcoming ball at Almack's - but Elizabeth struggled to concentrate. He had not said anything about his own feelings, had only offered her the hope that she would find what she wished for. Did that mean that he was entirely averse to such an idea? Would he have no desire to ask her to walk in the park or to take tea with him again? Her heart ached a little as she wondered if this was to be the last time she would be so in his company. Had she ruined their close acquaintance already, simply by telling him the truth? And why was the thought causing her heart so much pain?

CHAPTER EIGHT

"And are we to make for *this* carriage?"

Felix looked across at his men. These last few days, they had appeared increasingly disgruntled – although he could not understand why. He paid them the same as they had agreed, which meant that they must be displeased with his decision to no longer steal from those he stopped. Instead of choosing the very best of carriages to attack, he had chosen carriages that appeared a little less than grand. More often than not, Felix had found occupants within who were on their way to London for some reason *other* than to simply enjoy the Season. The men he had hired were dismayed that he had chosen to behave in such a fashion, although he found himself caring very little. After all, if he paid them what he promised - which he always did – then what should it matter what he did?

"If you do not wish to ride with me, then you need not do so." With a shrug, he turned back. "I am going to be doing whatever I think is best. Your assistance is required to stop the carriage but if you disagree with anything that I do, then you may turn around and return to London. I will find someone else to replace you."

Pushing his horse forward, his ears caught the murmurs and grumbles behind him, but Felix ignored it. If they continued, he was more than inclined to find someone else - perhaps *three* new riders – to join him. His eyes narrowed as he looked at the carriage, nodding slowly to himself.

"Yes, I think we should take this one."

Felix lifted his face to the wind. The sky was dark and the rain falling heavily but Felix did not care. His pursuit of the carriage was still something of a thrill, but he greatly enjoyed listening to the stories of those within. And seeing the astonishment on their faces when they realized that he was not about to steal from them, as he might have purported to do, was a thrill in itself. Certainly, he was not a highwayman like anyone had ever seen before, and that in itself was rather delightful. With a lift of his hand, he rode – and his men rode with him.

It took mere minutes for the coachman to stop.

"A wise decision!"

Laughing, his mask still fixed, Felix waved his pistol at the coachman. The man had stopped almost immediately and, given the heavy weariness on his face, it seemed that this was not the first time he had been stopped. Perhaps the man was already aware that such a thing might take place, and he had been prepared for it. Either that, or he had been driving for a little too long, and was weary to the bone.

"Wait there." Jumping down from his horse, he walked to the door and, rapping on the window, waited for it to open. When it did so, Felix could not help but grin, seeing the wide eyes and expressions of fear. He was looking forward to removing such an emotion from their faces. "Good afternoon."

The gentleman within scowled darkly at him.

"Be on your way."

Felix laughed.

"No, I think not. Instead, why do you not tell me a little about yourselves?" He chuckled, looking first at the gentleman who sat beside his wife. The lady herself was gripping his hand with tight fingers, her face white. "I always like to know a little about those I have stopped."

"I do not think that I am of any interest to you."

"All the same...." Felix held his pistol in one hand, allowing his gaze to drop to it for a moment. "I am waiting."

The gentleman's eyes flared, and then grew dark with anger.

"Very well." Sucking in a breath, he shook his head. "I am taking my wife and daughters to London in the hope of securing the younger a match."

"As are many others." Felix turned his attention to the two young women who were sitting on the other side of the carriage. They were clutching at each other, their faces equally white with fear. "I am sure that you will have no difficulty in securing a match for them *both,* for they are very beautiful young ladies."

"But certainly not suited to the proposal of a highwayman."

The sharp answer came from the matriarch and, with a chuckle, Felix turned his attention to her. The woman's face was white and as he looked at her, she closed her eyes tightly, her moment of courage seemingly gone.

"That is true." Lifting his eyebrows, he looked back at the gentleman. "Might I ask as to your identity?"

With yet another sigh, the gentleman gave it quickly, as if wishing this ordeal to be over as quickly as possible.

"I am Lord Stanfield."

Felix's heart lurched, his smile falling from his features. This was a gentleman with whom he was acquainted, albeit someone he had not seen in some time. In the dim light of the carriage – and with his mask on – Felix had not recognized Lord Stanfield, and immediately felt the urge to make certain that the gentleman knew of his true intentions.

"Well, Lord Stanfield." With a brief nod, he took a breath. "I do not mean to rob you. That is not my intention."

Lord Stanfield snorted.

"I can hardly believe that."

"And yet it is true - I have no intention of doing anything of the sort. You may find this a little hard to believe, but I am a fellow who is not in the least bit interested in stealing from you. Instead, I seek only to do some good, to see if I can offer aid in some way."

"I find that very difficult to believe."

The gentleman rolled his eyes, but Felix looked back at him with a broad smile on his face.

"All the same, it is true." Felix remarked with a grin. "Tell me, do you have a townhouse in London?"

"Indeed, we do." the lady remarked, sitting up more, although her eyes were still very wide, and she clearly believed that he was lying to them all. "What will you take from us? Please take whatever you wish and allow us to be on our way."

Felix sighed loudly.

"I truly have no intention of taking anything from you, whatever you have. All I wish for is a little conversation." How glad he was of his mask now! The last thing he wished for was to be identified by one of his acquaintances – a gentleman who had been acquainted with Felix's own father. From what Felix recalled, the man was honest, steadfast, and wise in every decision he made. Not the sort of gentleman he would dare lift a finger against. "You say that you seek out a match for your daughters?"

Lord Stanfield nodded, although his eyes remained a little narrowed.

"One is already betrothed," he stated, gesturing to the young woman who sat opposite him. "My eldest."

Felix leaned against the carriage door.

"Is that so?" He smiled at the lady. "My hearty congratulations." The young woman did not smile but rather flinched, as though he had injured her in some way. "And who is the fortunate gentleman?"

"It is Lord Hazelwood," Lady Stanfield spoke up again but, at this, Felix's smile fell to pieces. Lord Hazelwood was in London already, and Felix had seen him with his own eyes, dancing with any number of ladies and, unfortunately, pulling some unscrupulous ladies of the *ton* into dark corners. Lord Hazelwood was not a gentleman worthy of the daughter of Lord Stanfield.

Lord Stanfield frowned.

"You appear a little displeased. Surely you cannot have been thinking to steal my daughter away!"

Grimacing, Felix cleared his throat.

"No, I do not have any intentions of that," he remarked, attempting to keep his tone light, and reminding himself silently not to give himself away with any foolish remarks. "It is only that, I, being from London and all too aware of society and those within it - including those with deep pockets – recall that gentleman."

Lord Stanfield snorted in obvious ridicule.

"You meant to say that you know Lord Hazelwood? I can hardly believe it."

"Indeed I do." Felix shrugged his shoulders. "I am a little surprised to hear that your daughter is betrothed to him. Given what I witnessed, I was quite certain that he was involved with someone else."

"You lie!" Lady Stanfield sat bolt upright, one finger pointing out at him. "Your words are false. Lord Hazelwood is an excellent gentleman and would never treat my daughter in such a way!"

The urge to respond fought within him but, taking a moment, Felix merely looked away, maintaining as much nonchalance as he could.

"Very well." He said nothing more, looking away as though to say he did not care at all whether or not they believed him. "If you do not wish to trust my words, I shall not hold it against you."

There was a moment's pause.

"You speak very well for a highwayman."

Felix looked lazily back at Lord Stanfield, somewhat relieved that, with his mask, the gentleman had no way of realizing the truth about his identity.

"As I have said, I am a man well acquainted with all of society in London – from the poor to the wealthy." He shrugged again. "And I have a keen eye. I know what I saw."

Lord Stanfield let out a small huff, his face still holding a deep frown.

"And you would tell us this, no doubt, to disrupt us, to put us off from our journey, and to put a deep confusion into our souls. You intend to rob us still, I am sure."

"No, I do not." Allowing himself a smile, he stepped back. "In fact, be on your way. I have nothing to take from you today."

The gentleman exchanged a glance with his wife, then looked to his daughters. The first stared back at Felix. The second, however, soon dropped her head into her hands and began to sob.

"My dear Amelia, whatever is the matter?"

Lady Stanfield reached out to her daughter; Felix was suddenly forgotten.

"I have seen my betrothed with his arms around another."

She began to cry in earnest, and Felix's heart twisted a little in his chest. Evidently, she had seen more than she had ever been willing to say to her parents. He was glad now that he had spoken openly, even if it had caused the young lady pain.

"You mean to say that you saw Lord Hazelwood in such a position?" When the young lady only cried harder, Lord Stanfield closed his eyes tightly, his jaw set. "Why did you not say anything to me?"

The young woman began an explanation about how Lord Hazelwood had been so perfect a match and how he and Lady Stanfield had seemed to be so happy, but Felix did not listen to it. Instead, he simply stepped back and made to turn away, only to be faced by the three men he paid.

All began approaching him on foot, having left their horses behind and with two carrying their pistols also. Grey clouds gathered above Felix's head, and he glanced up at them, seeing the gathering storm clouds as a warning.

His stomach knotted.

"Whatever are you doing?"

"We are making sure that you take from these fine people." Stafford's jaw was tight. "We've spent days watching you doing nothing, waiting for you to take from them like you used to – but you won't. You have taken on the role of highwayman, but you're not doing anything about it."

"What does it matter what I do? "Felix exclaimed, suddenly angry. "I pay you to ride with me. That is all."

"But we want more," Connelly stated, but Felix only shook his head.

"Then I suggest you leave me and go to your own venture," Felix spat back, suddenly furious. How dare they turn upon him like this? "I pay you to obey my orders. If you think you can do a little better than I, might I suggest you leave my employ at once."

The third man chuckled.

"That's exactly what we're doing."

Felix's stomach dropped.

"We know you're a wealthy fellow," Stafford continued, darkly. "We may not know your title, but I'm sure someone in London would recognize your face."

"Except no one has ever seen my face," Felix retorted, only to realize this was a threat rather than a statement.

Did these men intend to unmask him and, thereafter blackmail him into doing whatever they wanted? If he did not pay them enough or do as they asked, then he would be revealed to all of society.

And to Lady Elizabeth.

Swallowing hard, Felix quickly took in his difficult situation. He was unbalanced, unguarded, alone against three men. How could he stand against them? What was it he could offer them that they did not already have?

"There is another choice." Connelly was grinning, his eyes glinting behind his mask. "You give us whatever we ask for and we don't reveal your face - or your name – to anyone."

Realizing he would have to summon great strength and show not even the smallest hint of weakness, Felix lifted his chin.

"I do not intend to reveal either to you, no matter your threats."

"Then you accept the consequences."

Without warning, Stafford stepped forward, one hand balled into a fist, but Felix dodged him quickly. His years of fencing, riding, and bouts of fighting had taught him to move quickly, always watching for what his opponent would do. His heart began to thud in his chest as he dodged one blow after another, realizing that, should they choose to, one of them might shoot him without warning.

Stafford was heavyset and slow, but Connelly and Griggs were quicker. A shove sent Stafford wheeling backward into Connelly, but Felix had barely a moment to catch his breath before kicking out hard at Griggs, knocking the pistol from his hand. There was no time to grasp it – not for either man. The fight was difficult for, the moment one man went down, another approached. His chances of succeeding were minimal indeed. He stepped back, assessing the situation, refusing to shoot his own pistol, unwilling to take the life of another. Connelly came again but Felix knocked the hand away, ducking his head as Grigg's fist swung towards him.

"Enough!"

Connelly and Griggs stepped back, leaving Stafford holding a pistol, which was aimed directly at Felix's heart.

"Take the mask from your face."

"No."

"Then if you will not, take what you can from this family and prove you are a highwayman. From now on, whatever you take will be shared between us – although your payments will continue."

Felix shook his head.

"I will not."

A tremor ran through him, but he lifted his chin.

"Very well." Stafford chuckled, then gestured to Griggs. "Take off your mask or we will take it from you."

A glance at his own pistol clutched in his hand, sent nothing but fear into his hand. If he raised it, he had no doubt Connelly would shoot him. Taking a breath, he fought to know what to do next, only to hear another soft click come from behind him.

"And you will step away." To Felix's astonishment, it was none other than Lord Stanfield, a pistol held around the carriage door. "You will leave the supposed highwayman alone."

Quickly, Felix lifted his own pistol only to see the confidence fade from Stafford's face. Evidently, the man had no intention of dying, and the threat of a pistol shot to the heart was difficult to accept. Griggs had no pistol any longer which meant the threat was all the greater.

"You are dismissed." Regaining himself a little, Felix sucked in air, his heart still pounding as he stood to his fullest height. "I do not need your services any longer. Take yourself from me. Oh, and Stafford? Leave your pistol behind."

The man's teeth gritted hard, his face red but, after some moments of silence, he accepted his loss. His head dropped and, eventually, he dropped the pistol and turned toward his horse. Griggs and Connelly followed.

Felix did not relax for a moment, keeping his own pistol trained on Stafford. The man was the instigator, the one who had pushed the other two forward, he was sure of it. He would not lower his pistol until they had ridden some distance away.

Eventually, the threat was over.

Felix sagged a little with relief.

"You did not have to do such a thing." Turning, he lifted one eyebrow when Lord Stanfield's pistol remained trained on him. "And nor do you have to do this."

Eyebrows lifted, Felix took a small step back, a prickling running up and down his spine as he looked into the man's eyes. Was Lord Stanfield about to shoot him? In taking on the guise of a highwayman, he had taken on the risk associated with it, for any man might seek to end his life or, at the very least, injure him for what he was doing. But accepting that was part of the thrill of what he did. This was to be expected, he knew that but, as he looked back into the barrel of the pistol, Felix's stomach dropped to the ground. Yes, it was a risk he had always accepted, but mayhap he had never taken it as seriously as he ought.

"Mayhap I sent those fellows away so I might shoot you myself." Lord Stanfield's eyes narrowed a fraction, only for him to take a breath. "All the same, I admit that you have done something of a service to me and my family, in being so honest about my daughter's betrothed."

The pistol wobbled for a moment and Felix held his breath, looking back into Lord Stanfield's eyes and, as he did so, gaining real clarity over what it was that he was doing, and everything associated with it. Was it all truly worth it?

"You did not seek to steal from us." One of the daughters spoke up as her father held the pistol steady again. "You were going to walk away."

"Yes." Felix shrugged his shoulders. "I confess that I have no intention of stealing from those that I stop. It makes me something of an unconventional highwayman, I know, but it is not what I do."

"I believe that I have heard of you," the gentleman muttered quietly. His pistol slowly dropped away, as if the decision in his own mind was already made. "There have been rumors of a highwayman who stops carriages but takes nothing from them. I assume that these stories are true? And that we now sit in the presence of that particular highwayman."

"It may well be so." Felix spread out both hands wide. "What I *shall* say is that I do not take for myself any longer and what I have taken, I am in the process of returning." A slight guilty nudge pushed into his heart as he recalled that he had not given Lady Elizabeth back her brooch. He would have to do so quickly, for it was one of the last things which he had to return and, at present, was pushed behind a particular book in his library. "In sincerity, I believe that the men who rode with me were becoming more and more frustrated with my actions."

Clearly a little surprised, the gentleman chuckled.

"Yes, I suppose they would be. Thus, because I realize who you are, I shall not shoot you. I do not refrain because of these stories, however. I refrain because you have done some good to my family, and because I believe that you were not to take anything from us. You defended us from the men who came, instead of joining them and thus I believe you speak with truthfulness upon your lips."

Felix inclined his head.

"Then I am grateful," he replied. "If I might, I shall take my leave. I wish you safe passage to London."

The gentleman smiled.

"Thank you. Good day."

With a heaviness in his steps which took him a little by surprise, Felix made his way back to his horse, watching as the carriage pulled away. His heart was heavy, not flooded with relief as he had expected it to be, but instead heavy with the realization of what he had been doing. He had been selfish, indulging a ridiculous whim to relieve his ennui.

It had been Lady Elizabeth, he realized, who had brought about a change in him. When he had met her, spoken with her, and smiled at her, then her tenacity and fire had caught him in a way that nothing else ever had. He had been unable to pull himself away from her since then, finding that his life was much more exciting simply because she was in it. Considering his heart, Felix let out a long sigh. No longer did he wish to steal and then return the items, nor even continue with his current good deeds. It was not worth the risk that came with it. Not now. What would he do if Lady Elizabeth were to hear the truth? If she realized that *he* had been the highwayman who had taken her brooch... and her lips, thereafter? Their acquaintance, such as it was, would come to an end.

Snatching in a breath, Felix's eyes closed, his stomach roiling at the thought. He could not bear to be separated from Lady Elizabeth. His only desire was for her company and her nearness – so why was he continuing with a foolish game, presenting a façade to the world, when that might pull them apart? It was unconscionable.

"Then it is done."

Taking a deep breath, Felix lifted his chin and set his shoulders. His time as a highwayman was at an end, a secret he would now keep buried in his past. He had no need for such activities to find a thrill any longer, no need to pursue any sort of excitement. His connection with Lady Elizabeth was exciting enough and, as he smiled quietly to himself at the mere thought of her, Felix silently swore to himself that, very soon, he would ask to court her, for that was his heart's desire.

CHAPTER NINE

"It is very strange."

"It is, I quite agree." Lady Yardley laughed softly and shook her head. "I cannot account for it! Every letter we have received, every account we have been offered, has been about a highwayman who does not steal but rather seeks to aid those he stops, in some way. I cannot imagine such a person, I confess."

"Neither can I." It was something of a shock and, with a frown, Elizabeth looked down at the letter again. It was one Lady Yardley had only just received, and the description within it was extraordinary. "Perhaps this highwayman is not the same as the one who acquainted himself with me."

"Oh, but I believe that it is." Lady Yardley's eyes danced. "The description of him is exactly the same as the man you have described. Tall, with flashing eyes hidden behind a dark mask. A hat – the same description as you have given – and dark hair curling at the edges. No indeed, my dear Elizabeth, I believe that this highwayman is the very same. It is only that somehow, and in some way, he has changed his ways from when he spoke with you."

Elizabeth still could not quite take it in. It was most extraordinary, for what sort of highwayman changed his ways in such an odd manner as this? He had taken her brooch, so why then would he not seek to do more? Why would he not desire everything that others could give him? It made very little sense, and Elizabeth passed one hand over her eyes for a moment, taking a breath as she attempted to come to an understanding of the situation.

"Mayhap it is that, in meeting you, he has decided to alter himself." Miss Millington smiled brightly as Elizabeth shot her a quick glance. "When you met him, no doubt you spoke with determination, and your words affected him in some way."

"Certainly, I did speak freely." Elizabeth frowned. "But why should my words make any particular difference? I am sure that many a person has spoken to him in such a way."

"Unless they have not." Lady Yardley shrugged. "Miss Millington might be correct. There could be something about you that caught his attention. After all, you said that you believed he was someone from the upper classes – so he has no need of the coin, and has chosen to mend his ways so that, if you meet again, you will think better of him."

The slight smile on her face made Elizabeth laugh as Miss Millington giggled.

"I hardly think a highwayman would develop a wish to improve himself, simply based upon me and my considerations."

Elizabeth laughed again, only to stop suddenly as the way he had kissed her came to mind. Absently, she touched her lips with one hand and did not see the way that Lady Yardley and Miss Millington exchanged a glance.

"Lady Yardley might well be correct!" Miss Millington giggled again, her eyes dancing. "This highwayman is a gentleman and, fearful you will not accept him if you discover the truth, now seeks to do good so that when the truth is revealed – for a gentleman cannot hide such a thing as that from any lady he desires – you will not think too badly of him."

This was all said with a slight twinkle in the lady's eye, which Elizabeth caught easily. She grinned.

"I do think that a little farfetched."

"As do I," Miss Millington replied with a chuckle. "But it is still within the realms of possibility."

"It is in the *far* realms of possibility, I think," Lady Yardley laughed. "But all the same, it seems as if this highwayman is not as he once was. I think…" Tilting her head, she nodded slowly, as if considering. "I think I shall publish *all* of these accounts. I think it only wise."

Elizabeth nodded.

"I agree." Something came to her and, biting her lip, she hesitated as Lady Yardley waited for her response. "Although I do not think it gives us any further way of identifying the highwayman. This last account - one from Lord and Lady Stanfield - states that the highwayman ended the betrothal between his daughter and a gentleman of the *ton*. At first glance, I thought it was that the highwayman had done something roguish, but it appears that the highwayman knew of this gentleman and was able to inform the young lady of what her betrothed had been doing in her absence." She shook her head, nibbling on the edge of her lip again for a moment. "Surely Lord Stanfield could have demanded that the highwayman remove his mask, that he make his features plain… but he did not. He could have shot him dead but, again, he did not."

"Because he identified that there is some good in this highwayman." Lady Yardley spoke softly. "There are always reasons behind the actions someone takes. I do not know precisely what this highwayman is doing, but whether he is a gentleman or not, there will be a reason for his change. There will be something that has shifted in his world, which now results in an altering of temperament and behavior. I am not suggesting that we need to discover what such a thing is. I only state that, from these accounts, we see that there *is* goodness within this person. He has a desire to aid, rather than to steal. And did you notice this also?" Getting up, she picked up one of the letters from the table and brought it back across to Elizabeth. "There are a few more than this, all stating the same," she finished quietly. "People who have had their precious items taken only to find them again some days or even weeks later. They cannot account for it, of course, being quite sure that the highwayman took such things from them. In some way, however, he appears to have given them back."

Elizabeth's eyebrows rose to her hairline.

"No, indeed I did not see this." Her heart twisted with a sudden painful jerk. "Though he has not returned my brooch as yet."

"He may."

Miss Millington rose, came across the room, and read the letter Elizabeth held in her hand, standing a little behind her.

"Does this not also suggest that it is someone from the higher classes? Someone who has no need for such wealth and therefore returns it?"

"Then why take it in the first place?" Elizabeth asked, still reading the few lines penned in the letter. "Why become a highwayman, if not to steal?"

There was a short pause.

"Simply for the sheer enjoyment of it? A diversion, almost – although not one I can condone."

Elizabeth looked up at her friend, her heart quickening.

"That is a wise thought." Pressing her lips together, she looked back at the letter. "Then am I to expect the return of my brooch at some unexpected moment?"

"You may have hope, certainly," Lady Yardley answered. "You must be careful to keep watch, Elizabeth. It may not require these accounts and letters for you to identify the highwayman."

It took a moment but, as she realized what Lady Yardley meant, Elizabeth caught her breath.

"You mean to suggest that he is already known to me," she said softly. "And therefore, at some moment I will find my brooch returned. When that happens, I will need to consider which gentlemen have been near me."

Lady Yardley nodded.

"That is my thinking at least," she murmured. "I shall put these accounts - all of them - in 'The London Ledger' over the next few publications. I hope we shall learn more about this highwayman."

"And have you anything else - or anyone else – you should like to enquire about?"

Miss Millington made her way back across the room, hiding her face and her expression from Elizabeth as she took her seat again. Confused, Elizabeth blinked.

"No." She spoke slowly. "Unless there is someone you think I ought to include?"

"I only meant Lord Winterbrook." Speaking plainly, Miss Millington grinned as Elizabeth looked quickly away. "He appears very eager for your company of late."

Upon hearing his name, such a heat ran through Elizabeth that she could not answer for a few moments. Struggling to know what to say, she looked first at Lady Yardley and then at her friend again.

"I - I believe that Lord Winterbrook has improved himself, or at least his impression upon me, a great deal since our first meeting." Speaking slowly, Elizabeth put a great deal of her heart into her response. "I thought him brash and a little arrogant at first and I will admit, there are still traces of that within his character. However, there is a tenderness about him that I had *not* expected, a kindness that runs through his character. He is most enjoyable company and, I will admit, very handsome as well!"

She finished with a giggle, the seriousness of their previous discussions now lifting from her. Lady Yardley chuckled, and Miss Millington laughed aloud, making Elizabeth smile all the more.

"That is good." Lady Yardley tipped her head a little. "Then might I ask if you have feelings for this gentleman? After what you have agreed upon with your friends – that you should all only wed gentlemen who care for you and for whom you care also – is it that Lord Winterbrook rouses such feelings within your heart?"

Elizabeth did not even need to consider.

"He and I have danced together, conversed together, laughed together, and walked together and I find I desire to do even more of all of these things." Her gaze went to Miss Millington. "My heart quickened even when you mentioned his name, so yes, I will admit that my heart is affected, and I am glad of it."

Miss Millington smiled.

"Would you accept him if he were to ask to court you?"

Pondering her friend's question, Elizabeth's gaze drifted idly for a few moments.

"I think I should need to know the state of his own heart

first," she answered carefully. "I have told him of my expectations when it comes to matrimony, and he is very well aware of them. Therefore, I hope that should such a thing take place, he will confess that his heart does pull towards me in return. If that is so, then I should be very glad to accept him."

With a small sigh, Miss Millington smiled gently.

"Then I hope that he will give you the answer you desire."

Elizabeth clasped her hands tight together, her heart turning over in her chest at the thought of what answer she might receive from him, should she have need to ask.

"As do I, Miss Millington. As do I."

∽

"Yet again, you have taken my waltz, Lord Winterbrook."

Elizabeth's smile tilted up at Lord Winterbrook though, to her surprise, his eyes widened a little and his mouth did not curve as she had expected.

"Do you mean to say that you would prefer someone else to stand up with you?" Putting one hand to his heart, he inclined his head. "Forgive me, I ought not to have been so selfish. If you desire someone else to waltz with you, then I would be glad to step back."

"No, indeed you misunderstand me." Laughing, she reached one hand out and put it on his arm for a moment. "The truth is, Lord Winterbrook, that I am truly delighted that you have taken my waltz, even if it is for the third time. It is only a small concern which lingers."

"Which is?"

"I worry that some may remark upon it."

Instantly, brightness flooded his expression and he

grinned, now returning to the confident gentleman she knew him to be.

"And what if they *should* do so?" He lifted one shoulder in a half-shrug. "I should not care one whit if society believes I am caught up with you, Lady Elizabeth, for indeed, that is the truth."

Heat burned flames up Elizabeth's veins, suddenly ignited by his words. Staring at him, she allowed her smile to fall to one side, only for him to step closer. A little startled, she made to pull her hand away, but he caught it, his fingers lacing through her own, albeit in a guarded manner, and only for a few moments.

"This is not the way I wished to have such a conversation, but I fear it will not wait." Taking a breath, he lifted his chin just a little. "Lady Elizabeth, I have a fervent desire to court you, if you would wish to be so courted." A gentle red rose in his face, his eyes no longer holding hers but darting around her face. "Mayhap I ought to go to your mother to ask such a thing but, given that she is absent this evening and given that my patience has worn thin, I cannot help but express my desire to you alone. I want very much to court you, Lady Elizabeth. It has been my desire for some time, I believe, growing quickly and without restraint." A sudden frown marred his expression, and he dropped his head. "Forgive me for being tardy with my request."

Elizabeth's breath was quickening but her response was ready, as if the words had been waiting at the door of her lips.

"I do not think you tardy, nor overly hasty, Lord Winterbrook. Instead, I think you have asked at the most opportune time." A smile began to lift the edges of his mouth, but she quickly continued, remembering what she had said to Lady Yardley only the day before. "However, there is something that would prevent me from accepting you. My own desire is to marry a gentleman who will love me, as I have already told you. I will not enter into a courtship where there is no affection. For if there are no feelings of the heart at this present juncture, then I highly doubt there will be any hope of it within matrimony, should courtship lead to that."

Her own heart cried out with a sudden sorrow, pained by a pang of regret, for what if she were the one who, alone, held a great emotion for Lord Winterbrook? What if he did not return her affection? Elizabeth was sure that her heart would break for she would have to watch him walk away, aware that she had been offered a small chance of happiness, but that her own determination had stolen it from her.

No, it would be all the more painful to marry a gentleman who did not love me while I loved him in return.

"I do recall your statement as regarded this..." Lord Winterbrook's expression was steady. He was not smiling but nor was he frowning. "I respect your standing in this matter, and pray do trust me when I say that I would not have asked you this question had I not such feelings myself."

Elizabeth looked back into his eyes and felt her heart leap with such joy that it stole her breath away, leaving her almost numb with happiness. This was what she had wanted for a long time, what she had been hoping for, searching for, over many a year. Now, in her third Season, it seemed as though Lord Winterbrook was to be the one who answered her silent prayers, her fervent hopes, and the desperate longings of her heart.

"You... You care for me."

The words were barely whispered, but in response, Lord Winterbrook smiled and nodded.

"I do indeed." Leaning down towards her, his smile grew all the more. "And you care for me."

There was no flush to her cheeks, nor a wave of embarrassment which had her looking away from him. Instead, she held his gaze steadily and found his hand again, heedless of those who might see them in such close proximity.

"Yes."

"Then, might I ask," Lord Winterbrook murmured, holding her hand tightly. "Whether you intend to accept my offer of courtship?"

Wishing that she might have the freedom to throw herself into his arms and wrap herself as close to him as she could, Elizabeth satisfied herself by squeezing his fingers.

"I do accept, Lord Winterbrook. I accept it with my whole heart."

CHAPTER TEN

"I hear that you are now courting Lady Elizabeth."

Felix looked at Lord Bramwell.

"You heard correctly."

He said nothing more as they walked through London, even though he was all too aware of Lord Bramwell's hard stare.

"You did not think to tell me of your intentions before you asked her?"

Felix frowned.

"Why should I need to inform you?"

"Because I am your friend," came the sharp response. "But then again, you have been rather secretive of late. Mayhap I ought to have expected this silence."

With a sigh, Felix looked over at his friend.

"I have not been secretive."

"Certainly, you have," Lord Bramwell stated, in a tone that demanded that Felix not argue. "You have done nothing but hide the truth from me, pretending that she is nothing but one of your many acquaintances. In truth, I find you very confusing indeed."

Frowning, Felix slowed his steps.

"In what way?"

"Well," Lord Bramwell responded, quickly, "First, you tell me that you are bored and that you intend to find some way to entertain yourself, but you will not tell me *what* that entertainment is. Thereafter, you say nothing about Lady Elizabeth, even though I have been quite certain that you have been desirous of her company for some time. Then I hear from another acquaintance that you are now courting the lady!"

Wincing at the slight edge of his friend's tone, Felix bit back his first, sharp response.

Perhaps Lord Bramwell truly was a little frustrated that Felix had kept so much to himself.

After all, we do share a good many things.

"I see." With a small shrug, he looked away. "I am sorry that I have pained you by my silence, though you ought now to be grateful for it."

Lord Bramwell's eyes narrowed.

"In what way?"

"Because," Felix responded, truthfully, "I have been selfish and acted in a most inappropriate manner. I have taken risks I ought not to have done and, in doing so, have found myself embarrassed by my own foolish choices." His friend shot him a quick look. "I do not say any of this as a pretense. I speak honestly and openly, for it is all I can offer you at present. Perhaps I ought to have spoken to you about Lady Elizabeth before now, but the truth was that I have found myself rather surprised that I should *ever* have any particular feelings as regards any young lady, I did not think, even in courtship, that my heart would pull towards someone so."

Stating this aloud had him blinking in surprise over just

how much he felt and, given Lord Bramwell's wide eyes, it seemed he was just as astonished also.

"Then... you are considering matrimony?" Lord Bramwell's tone held nothing but surprise. "Even though, at the start of the Season, you were quite determined not to do so?"

Felix chuckled, then passed one hand over his eyes, letting out a low groan.

"I do not know what I intend." He dropped his hand back to his side. "The truth is, I am very confused and uncertain as to what I want. The only thing I am fully aware of at present is that I want the company of Lady Elizabeth as frequently as I can have it."

Lord Bramwell sucked air through his teeth.

"Good gracious." Seeing Felix's lifted brows, he shrugged. "It seems as though you might very well be falling in love with the lady, which is certainly all the more surprising. Even I did not believe that you would ever even *consider* such a thing." This latter part was said with a broad grin, and Felix laughed, shaking his head as Lord Bramwell grinned back at him, the edge of seriousness gone from their words. "In hindsight, I should not be too frustrated over your lack of explanation about Lady Elizabeth." After some moments of silence, Lord Bramwell cleared his throat but kept his eyes turned to the path ahead rather than looking at Felix. "There has been something I ought to have told you also. I have kept it from you deliberately, however."

"Oh?"

Attempting to make light of what was a serious consideration, Lord Bramwell shrugged and sniffed.

"Nothing of any great significance, really. It is only that I am... considering marriage also."

These last few words came out in a rush and Felix found himself smiling.

"Truly?"

"Truly." Lord Bramwell glanced at Felix, then tugged his gaze away again – but not before Felix had spotted the redness of Lord Bramwell's face. "I was acquainted with Lord Ruthven back in Eton and unfortunately, was not in the least bit surprised to hear how he had treated Miss Whitford. He has always been a selfish fellow, even in Eton. I find her quite charming and, therefore, I have not only asked her for her hand, but also made it plain that I intend to speak to Lord Ruthven myself. Firmly, if I have to."

Felix's eyebrows leaped fully towards his hairline.

"You mean to say that you are betrothed?"

His surprise could not be hidden and, when his friend looked at him, Felix let out a bark of laughter.

"It is no laughing matter!" Lord Bramwell threw up his hands. "I am quite serious. I believe Miss Whitford and I are an excellent fit for each other and will do very well."

Rather than laugh any further, Felix merely stopped, turned, and reached to grasp his friend's hand, shaking it firmly although a broad smile still spread across his face.

"I am very pleased for you. *Very* pleased for you indeed. In truth, when I first met the lady, I did wonder whether or not she might do for you." He tipped his head. "It is good to know that I was correct."

Lord Bramwell made to snort but ended up grinning.

"You can be very proud of your achievement – though I do hope, in all sincerity, that you will be able to find yourself betrothed also, very soon."

"Thank you." Felix smiled. "I have thought to host a soiree next week. Might you wish to attend?"

"I certainly should." Lord Bramwell grinned, his eyes

dancing "As long as my betrothed is also permitted an invitation."

Slapping Lord Bramwell on the shoulder good-naturedly, Felix chuckled.

"Of course she is invited," he promised. His eyes slid away from his friend and, with a broad grin, he stepped away from him. "And if you will excuse me, I can see that the object of my own desires has just now come into the park. Do excuse me."

The way that Lady Elizabeth's eyes seemed to find him, the smile lighting up her features when he approached, made Felix's heart leap with happiness. It was foolishness to pretend that he had no affection for the lady or that he wasn't becoming overwhelmed by her, for the thudding of his heart when he drew closer to her was something he could not ignore.

I do not deserve her attentions.

She was all sweetness, and he, a scoundrel. Lady Elizabeth did not know of his highwayman ways and, with that thought, his smile began to fade, his step slowing a little. Having decided to give up his escapades as a highwayman, could he still court her without telling her the truth? Even if he found a way to return her brooch, would it be enough?

And what if we marry?

His heart began to slow to a dull thud. Would he truly be so easily able to keep what he had done a secret from her for the rest of their days? He did not think that he could. Such a thought had not troubled him before, but now it began to come to the fore in his mind, and he grew all the more concerned. Courtship was the first step towards betrothal and from betrothal to marriage. They would be as close as two people could possibly be. Would it be right for him to keep such a thing from her? If he held a true affection for her as he claimed, then surely he had to be honest.

"At first, you seemed pleased to see me but as you approached, that smile fled from your face." Lady Elizabeth tilted her head as her mother stopped a short distance away, allowing them a private conversation but keeping a careful eye on her daughter at the same time. "Are you quite well, Lord Winterbrook?"

"I am quite well." He cleared his throat roughly. "It is only that I have had some thoughts of late and I am a little confused by them."

Lady Elizabeth's smile did not return.

"Might I be so bold as to ask what these thoughts are about?"

"They are not to do with my affection for you, if that is what concerns you, my dear Lady." The way her smile returned told him that this was precisely what she had been worried about. "No, Lady Elizabeth, it is something more." Taking a breath, he shook his head a little, uncertain as to what it was that he was going to say. The thoughts of matrimony, of his highwayman ways, of her brooch, and his affection for her ran all through his mind, tangling up his senses. "At the start of this London Season, I confess to you, I found it all to be rather dull. I was in something of a misery in fact, albeit until I met you."

Pink came to her cheeks, her blue eyes alive as she smiled up at him.

"You are very charming indeed, Lord Winterbrook."

"And yet I speak the truth." Swallowing a lump in his throat, he turned and offered her his arm. "Might you walk with me?"

A great tumult arose in his mind as she accepted him. Did she have any awareness of just how her nearness affected him? A gentle scent of lavender wound around him – whether from her or the gardens, he did not know – but it only added to his confusion rather than allowing any sort of clarity.

"Are you quite well, Lord Winterbrook?"

"I am *more* than well." Speaking rather more urgently than he had intended, Felix licked his lips. "Sometimes I fear there is more to my character – and my past – than you are aware of. I am considering whether or not to share such things with you."

Lady Elizabeth smiled sweetly, seemingly entirely unperturbed by his remarks.

"I suggest, Lord Winterbrook, that if you wish to speak to me about something, then you do so, rather than allow it to weigh upon you so. However, people can change, and I am also aware that many gentlemen have, in the past, behaved differently than they do at present and, if it is so with you, then I do not think that you need share such things with me. In fact, I think it is wiser to keep such things to yourself. I do not want my present considerations of you to be at all affected."

All the more confused within himself, Felix took a breath, not returning her smile.

"I see."

"Unless it is something pressing heavily upon your conscience." Her smile grew faint. "I should not urge you to refrain then."

Felix was about to begin, only to shake his head. The words would not come, his heart refusing to permit him to speak freely. The fear of being torn from her, that she would step away from him, was much too great. It bound him to her and tied his mouth closed at the same time.

His breath came out in a sigh.

"It is nothing of great consequence," he said, finally, with a smile that did not stretch as widely across his face as he had hoped. "I shall soon be sending out invitations to an evening soiree. I do hope that you will be able to attend?"

Lady Elizabeth squeezed his arm, seemingly relieved that the conversation had altered.

"But of course! I could not refuse such a wonderful invitation. I do not think that I have ever been to your townhouse as yet. I am already looking forward to it."

"I will be very glad to show you my townhouse." Pushing away his tumultuous thoughts, Felix fixed his mind on the upcoming soiree, rather than allowing himself to become lost in confusion. "It will be a fairly small soiree, but those who attend will know that we are courting. I hope that you do not mind such a thing?"

"No indeed!" Lady Elizabeth laughed, then tucked herself a little closer to him. "I am very glad to be seen on your arm." She smiled just a little, her expression soft. "My heart is glad also."

Felix let out a slow breath. The truth was, he was becoming more and more enamored of Lady Elizabeth with every moment that they spent together, and this moment was no exception. Her beautiful smile, her tender words, the softness of her lips, the warmth in her eyes... it was all he could do not to pull her into his arms. Gathering himself, he paused in their walk, turned, and grasping her hand with his fingers, lifted it to his lips. Lingering there for a little longer than required, Felix discovered that his heart was so full of affection for the lady, he could not even hope to find the words to express it.

"I find you utterly wonderful in every aspect," he told her, seeing the flush which came into her cheeks. "You steal my breath from me."

"I thank you."

Her words were breathless, her eyes melding to his.

"I do not say such things to flatter you, but because my heart demands that I speak them. I mean every word, Lady Elizabeth. I find that my heart is unable to set you aside for even a moment. You are always in my thoughts, always in my heart. Indeed, Lady Elizabeth, my heart is yours."

Her eyes widened just a little, but before she could respond, he slipped her hand through his arm, turned, and then continued to walk.

Felix's smile faded to a frown. If he truly meant those words, which he was certain he did, then how could he hide what he had done with her brooch? At the same time, how could he even *think* of speaking honestly, knowing that it could push her away from him for good? He dared not even allow himself to think of what it would be like to lose her company, her smile, her laughter, her joy from his life. But if he loved her, could he truly keep such a secret to himself?

CHAPTER ELEVEN

"He has a beautiful townhouse, does he not, Mama?"

It was something of a rarity for Lady Longford to step out into society or attend any occasion whatsoever. Having spent the last few weeks resting, on this occasion, she had been very eager to attend the soiree. Elizabeth was happy about it for, while she had been very glad of Lady Yardley's accompanying her, there had been a sense of absence when her mother had not been standing beside her. How glad she was now that Lady Longford was feeling well enough to step out with her. To Elizabeth's mind, this was one of the most important occasions of the Season thus far.

"It is very pleasant." Lady Longford smiled warmly. "Lord Winterbrook is an excellent fellow, it seems, even though his title is a little less than that of your father."

Elizabeth let out a quiet chuckle.

"Mama, you know that such things mean very little to me."

"Yes, however, they mean a great deal with your father and I." The quick response came with a warm smile. "But he is wealthy enough and certainly seems to be amiable also. As you know, I have written to your father, but I am certain that he will be more than content with a betrothal, should it come." Elizabeth clutched her mother's arm for a moment, betraying herself with that response. Her mother smiled softly, turning to face Elizabeth as they stood to one side of Lord Winterbrook's drawing room. Lady Longford tilted her head just a little. "You *are* aware that such a thing might very well take place soon, are you not?" she asked softly. "That is precisely the reason he wishes to see you, to be further acquainted with you. It is because you are the object of his affections, and therefore, he expects that courtship might very well lead to betrothal. It is something you desire yourself, is it not?"

"I... I did not think it would be something considered so soon." Elizabeth blinked quickly, wishing that she had remembered to bring her fan. In truth, she had been so delighted with the beginnings of their courtship that she had given very little consideration to the idea that Lord Winterbrook might propose to her soon after. Her heart was already engaged with his, certainly, and from what he had said to her only last week, she believed that he felt the same. But the thought of a proposal, of a betrothal, was so very exciting, it left her a little breathless. *What if he is hoping to propose to me this very evening?* "I know what my answer would be, Mama."

Lady Longford smiled at her.

"I am most glad to hear it," she answered quietly. "But does it fulfill your requirements, Elizabeth?" Her eyebrows lifted in confusion as her mother laughed softly. "Recall that you stated that you would not wed a gentleman who did not care for you, and for whom you did not care in return. Does that still stand?"

"Indeed, it does," Elizabeth answered, her heart swelling with happiness. Now, she could confirm to her mother that what she had been seeking, she had found. "I have already found what I hoped for in Lord Winterbrook, and I am altogether grateful for it."

"Then I am *very* glad." Lady Longford squeezed Elizabeth's hand for a moment. "You deserve such happiness, my dear girl. You have been determined, and you have sought out this for yourself with unwavering resolve. I am delighted that you have succeeded in your desire."

"Thank you, Mama."

Elizabeth took a deep breath and smiled at Lady Yardley, who was approaching. This evening was to be an excellent one, she was sure, for already, she was surrounded by friends and family. Her heart was filled with such a sense of overwhelming happiness, it was as if she could not quite take a full breath. If he were to ask her even this very evening, then Elizabeth would be more than glad to accept his hand.

"Good evening." Lady Yardley inclined her head, coming to join them. "How good it is to see you both. And how do you fare, Lady Longford?" Elizabeth smiled as her mother and Lady Yardley began a conversation. That smile soon faded as she realized that Lady Yardley was acting in a slightly unusual manner. She was looking at Elizabeth with short, sharp glances as if wanting to attract her attention without letting her mother become aware of it. Whatever could this mean? "And you, Lady Elizabeth, are you quite well this evening?"

Frowning, Elizabeth nodded.

"Yes, I am, thank you."

Lady Yardley's eyebrows lifted.

"I see." After a moment, she smiled. "That is good."

A little confused and wondering if Lady Yardley had expected a different answer. Elizabeth's forehead lined for a moment.

"Is there some reason I might not be?"

Lady Yardley only managed a small smile.

"I assume that Lady Sherbourne and Miss Millington have not managed to speak to you as yet this evening?" Her tone was amiable enough, but Elizabeth caught that the words meant something more. "Might you wish to go and join them? They are just a little over there."

With a nod, Elizabeth excused herself, making her way quickly over to where Miss Millington and Lady Sherbourne were standing. When she approached, their wide eyes and tight lips gave her no clear indication as to what the concern was, only that there was something wrong.

"Good evening." Her gaze darted from one to the other. "Might you tell me what your concern is? Lady Yardley has asked me to come and join you, but I do not understand why."

Her friends exchanged a glance and then Miss Millington put one hand on Elizabeth's arm.

"It is only that... There's something a little odd in the library."

"In the library?" Elizabeth repeated, frowning. "Whatever do you mean?"

Miss Millington licked her lips.

"I am at times a little curious, and I confess that in this situation I was very curious indeed! I do very much enjoy seeing the sort of things that other gentlemen and ladies have within their homes, and given that Lord Winterbrook has opened up his drawing room, library, and parlor to us, I did have a prolonged perusal in his rooms."

"Which is quite understandable."

Eager to reassure her friend that she did not think ill of her because of this, Elizabeth spoke quickly, but Miss Millington shook her head.

"What I discovered," Miss Millington continued, her voice so soft that Elizabeth had to strain to hear it, "Was a particular book that caught my attention. It was in the corner of the library on one of the shelves, but it jutted out a little and I could not understand why. This is where I state that you must forgive my curiosity, for I stepped forward and made to push it back into place, but it would not move." Swallowing, she lifted her gaze to Elizabeth, then turned it away again. "Something was behind it and, upon discovering a small black velvet bag, I could not help but see what was within." Still confused about what her friend was talking about, Elizabeth merely waited for the final explanation. "I am sure," Miss Millington finished, her head dropping forward, "I am sure that I found your brooch, Elizabeth."

Shock ran like ice through her veins.

"My brooch?" she repeated, stupidly. "What do you mean?"

"We may very well be wrong," Lady Sherbourne interjected quickly. "Miss Millington showed it to me, and we do both think it appears very similar to the one you call your own, that is all."

"And, recall, I did see you wearing it last Season," Miss Millington added. "I do not think that I would have recognized it otherwise."

Elizabeth took a breath. Her stomach was churning this way and that, but she shook her head, confident in Lord Winterbrook.

"I am certain that you are mistaken, although I appreciate your concern. I trust Lord Winterbrook. Why ever would he have my brooch?"

"Why indeed?" Lady Sherbourne offered her a quick smile, but it faded soon afterward. "Perhaps we are quite mistaken. It would be very strange indeed if he *did* have your brooch."

A sudden fear wrapped itself around Elizabeth's heart.

I cannot know for certain unless I see it.

With a forced smile, she gestured to the door.

"Might we make our way to the library so that I might look at this brooch for myself?"

Miss Millington nodded.

"Of course. I am sure that we are mistaken. It would not make any sense at all for Lord Winterbrook to have it."

"None whatsoever," Elizabeth responded with a firmness that she did not feel.

Slowly, pieces were sliding towards each other, beginning to produce a clarity within her heart that she had not seen before.

Her strength beginning to waver, she followed her friends to the library. It was not overly crowded with other guests, for which she was grateful. As she trailed after Miss Millington, her heart began to pound, her breath coming in short snatches, and she was suddenly afraid of what she would see, and what it would mean.

"Here it is."

It took a few moments to find the book she had been looking for, but once it was found and pulled back, Miss Millington stepped aside to allow Elizabeth to look. Reaching out, her fingers ran lightly over the brooch and, pulling it forth, she gazed down at it.

This cannot be!

She did not have to take more than one glance to know it was her own. This piece was well known to her, for how often had her eyes run over every inch of it, taking in every sparkling piece? Yes. This *was* her brooch, her heirloom, and the one which had been taken from her by the highwayman.

Lady Sherbourne was biting her lip as Elizabeth looked up. Miss Millington was dancing from one foot to the other.

"Surely it could not be..."

Miss Millington's voice faded as she looked into Elizabeth's eyes, perhaps seeing the same fears there which she evidenced with her words.

"Yes, this is my own." Elizabeth's voice was shaking. "I dare not even imagine what..." Her eyes closed and she swayed a little. "Yet I must know for certain." Her mind fixed upon an idea that would not let her free. Whirling around, her skirts flying, she went in search of Lord Winterbrook, the brooch tucked tightly into her hand. With great strides she went through each room, only to discover him in the parlor, speaking with another gentleman. At that moment, no other people were in the room, for which she was grateful. When Elizabeth entered without a chaperone, both gentlemen's eyebrows lifted. "Pray excuse me, Lord Bramwell."

Elizabeth knew that she was being bold, but she found that she did not care about any suggested impropriety. The gentleman blinked in surprise but upon seeing her lift her chin, he hurried quickly from the room, leaving Elizabeth to push the door closed.

"Lady Elizabeth." Lord Winterbrook, who stood by the fireplace, turned towards her with eyebrows lifted high. "I..." His gaze went to the closed door. "Are you quite well? I am sorry that I have not yet greeted you. It was not my intention to delay."

Elizabeth did not allow him to finish speaking. Tears fell as she stepped close to him, put her hand on his shoulder, and pressed her lips to his.

She knew in an instant.

Lord Winterbrook was the highwayman who had kissed her and taken her brooch. The way his lips felt, the strength of him under her fingers, even the scent of him near her – it was all the same. How could she have been so entirely blind?

Tears dampened her cheeks and, with the kiss, fell to his also. With another sob, she stepped back, one hand to her eyes, covering them to hide the sight of him.

"Lady Elizabeth." Lord Winterbrook's voice was hoarse, his hand finding hers, gently tugging it from her eyes. "Whatever is the matter?"

The door behind them opened suddenly, but Elizabeth did not so much as glance at it. Instead, she held Lord Winterbrook's hand and, her chest heaving with unspent sobs, opened her hand and showed him the brooch.

Lord Winterbrook's face fell.

CHAPTER TWELVE

"Whatever is the meaning of this?"
Felix could not understand whether it was Lady Elizabeth who had spoken or someone else entirely. Blood was roaring in his ears, his eyes fixed on the brooch in her hand, horrified now that she had found it. Yes, he had been seeking to give it back to her but, in truth, had not considered it particularly urgent. He had become so transfixed with the closeness of their acquaintance that he had set it to one side in his mind.

How did she find it?

From what he remembered, he had placed it in the library, within a small velvet bag behind a book, and had never once imagined that anyone would discover it – not even his staff. Servants whispered and he could not allow any of them to know of what he had been doing as the highwayman. Now it appeared as though guilt and shame were to bring down heavy consequences upon his head.

"Are you betrothed?" The voice spoke again, and Felix dragged his eyes away from the brooch, finding himself gazing into the face of another. "Is *that* the reason you are in here alone with the door shut tight? Or must I fetch Lady Longford?"

Felix blinked rapidly, looking into the eyes of Lady Dresden who was, unfortunately, one of the worst gossips in all of London. What was he to say? Lady Elizabeth had done the most extraordinary thing, first striding into his parlor, then demanding that Lord Bramwell take his leave and, finally, pressing a kiss to his lips. But now her reputation would have to be salvaged in some way, and the only thing he could think to do to protect Lady Elizabeth was to concur with Lady Dresden.

"There is a reason."

His voice was gruff as Lady Dresden caught her breath, her eyes sparkling.

"Then you *are* betrothed!"

"I was just about to ask the lady, in fact," he stated, demanding silently that his smile linger. "Lady Dresden, I know that you will be most eager to spread this news, but might you give me only one more minute alone with Lady Elizabeth? I have not yet asked her, and I should very much like to be able to do so before I present her to my friends and acquaintances as my betrothed."

Lady Dresden's eyes lit up. She nodded, clapped her hands in evident joy, and stepped away, ready to revel in the fact that *she* had been the one to first find out about the betrothal.

"I will not marry you."

Lady Elizabeth's spat those words towards him, her eyes sharp but still glassy with tears. Felix's heart broke asunder. He was the cause of this. He was the reason for her sorrow, for her sadness, for her broken heart. By keeping this from her, he had managed to ruin himself entirely in her eyes, and yet the problem which was now between them was entirely insurmountable if they did not wed.

"You must." Taking a deep breath, he threw out both hands, seeing her scowl at him. "I know you have no wish to, and no doubt you will require a great deal of explanation, but after what Lady Dresden has just seen, we *must* marry. I will not have your reputation ruined for my sake, not after I have broken so much already."

"A noble desire." The irony in her tone lashed out at him, hard, and Felix winced, accepting that he deserved her censure but struggling to accept it nonetheless. "I would rather my reputation be ruined entirely so I did not have to marry you."

With a sigh, Felix took a step towards her, hating to see her flinch.

"And yet it must be so," he said quietly. "Far be it from me to advise you but, in this, you must be wise and cautious. We *must* marry. The rumors will begin the moment we step out of this room and, if we are not betrothed, then it will be a scandal. Your father's name will be affected – and the reputation of your sisters, even though they are already wed, will also be tarnished. It is for the best for everyone for us to marry, even if you do not wish to do so." Another step brought him to within a handsbreadth of her. "I will give you whatever you wish, even if it be your own estate where you might live far from me. I will give you all that you desire. Do not ruin yourself over this, I beg of you."

Pink came into her cheeks as she looked back at him. Her lips were trembling, no words coming from her and the sadness in her eyes was almost more than he could bear. Silence filled the room. Felix closed his eyes, swallowing hard, silently praying that he would not be the cause of Lady Elizabeth's ruination.

"And how would you pay for such an estate?" Finally breaking the quiet, Lady Elizabeth's voice was filled with ice. "Is it from the things which you have taken from others?"

He shook his head.

"I have never kept anything I have taken."

"Apart from my brooch."

Shame drew his head forward.

"Apart from your brooch," he admitted softly. "After I met you, I swear, I never took another item from anyone. As regards your brooch, I had the intention of returning it to you – as I had returned every item before that. I did not know how to do so, given that our connection was becoming so warm, and my heart so involved."

Her broken laughter shattered the room, sending shards of shame to pierce him.

"How can I trust a word you have said to me?" Her tone was harsh, burning words scalding his skin. "You said you cared for me but how can you do so when *you* took this brooch from me? You knew how much it meant to me and still you did not return it. You had ample opportunity to do so, but you did not."

Accepting her words, Felix's shoulders dropped low. Lady Elizabeth was quite correct. Yes, he had needed to put the brooch back into her possession but instead, he had focused on his connection to her, chasing away the idea for fear it might drive them apart.

"I swear to you, I did have an intention to return it, though it was not at the forefront of my mind." Admitting this aloud, he reached to touch her hand with his, but she shuddered and pulled away. Felix's heart tore all over again.

"If you might consider allowing me to explain all to you, then I would be most grateful. I fully understand that you might have very little desire to do anything of the sort, however, in which case I shall respect that also."

Her eyes now clear of tears, but her cheeks still a little flushed, Lady Elizabeth looked at him.

"And yet you still expect me to betroth myself to you?"

Having no other answer, Felix put out both hands.

"I do not know. I shall leave that decision with you." Gesturing to the door, he sidestepped her as he made for it. "But we must take our leave. We have been in here for too long, alone, already. Please."

The moment he opened the door, there were about a dozen expectant faces looking at him – including that of Lord Bramwell. Felix said nothing, not even smiling, but instead turning his attention to Lady Elizabeth. Taking a moment, Lady Elizabeth held her head high and walked to the door, her shoulders stiff and her face expressionless. Felix held her gaze, watching her expression change when her eyes turned toward those who were waiting. Her eyes flared as she took in their obvious expectation, her face losing its last hint of color as she glanced toward him.

Felix held his breath.

"We are betrothed."

Her voice was broken with emotion and while everyone else smiled and cheered and even yelled with evident delight, Felix was all too aware that Lady Elizabeth felt nothing of joy or happiness. She had said those words simply to protect herself, and to protect her family's reputation. Had she had any choice in the matter, she would have rejected him outright and been perfectly right to do so. He would have been injured, his heart painful with regret, but he would have deserved it.

"My hearty congratulations!" Lord Bramwell appeared by Felix's side and slapped him on the shoulder. "I must confess that I was rather surprised when Lady Elizabeth threw herself into the parlor in that manner. I did not expect it in the least!"

"Nor did I." Felix dropped his head, running one hand over his eyes, his heart so heavy he could not help but speak. "Bramwell, I have entangled myself in a dire situation. It is full of thorns and briars, and I do not know how I am to extricate myself from it."

Lord Bramwell blinked, his smile frozen to his features.

"I thought you would be very glad indeed to have betrothed yourself to Lady Elizabeth. Had you not planned to do so?"

"It was not my intention when she arrived." Felix swallowed hard, his throat rough, and lifted his gaze back to his friend. "We must become betrothed to protect her reputation. While I will say, it was extraordinary what she did in marching into the room in such a manner, it came about because of something *I* have done." Something coiled around his throat as Lord Bramwell frowned. "I have done something so very wrong, I do not think that she will ever forgive me. We will marry, yes, but it will not be a happy union. I am not what she wanted, nor what she hoped for – and certainly not who she deserves. I have taken all her dreams and torn them into pieces, and ruined her chances of finding what she promised herself."

"And what is that."

Sighing heavily, Felix let his gaze drift to where Lady Elizabeth was being embraced by her mother.

"She sought a gentleman who loved her, and whom she loved in return," he said softly. "And I may love her, Bramwell, my heart may be filled with her, but I do not think that she will ever be able to love me. And that is something I fully deserve."

∼

THE SOIREE HAD ENDED some hours ago, but Felix had not been able to retire. His head was far too full of thoughts, swirling and tormenting him in equal measure and thus, he now found himself wandering through the dark streets of London with never a care as to where he went.

His betrothal to Lady Elizabeth ought to be a source of great joy, but instead, it brought nothing but guilt. How could he tie himself to a young lady such as her, so beautiful, so kind and sweet, when he was nothing but a scoundrel? The weight of his previous choices hung heavily upon him, as did his awareness that now she saw him as he truly was – a scoundrel who had done nothing other than steal from her and thereafter, attempted to steal her heart also, without ever being true to her about who he was, what he had done, and how he had injured her. The grief that brought him was immense, and yet the consequences of it, he knew, were entirely of his own making. Quite what he was to do now, Felix had very little idea. His heart still yearned for her, desperate now to make amends, in some way, for what he had done, to prove that he loved her still. Yet even the thought of speaking to her, of trying to explain to her what he had done and the reasons behind it, seemed futile. His explanation that he had been bored and dulled by society was weak, showing him to be nothing but selfish, which, Felix realized, was precisely what he had been.

"I am nothing but a fool."

Sweeping darkness seemed to answer him as a cloud pulled itself in front of the moon, blocking out the dim light.

Scowling, Felix trudged forward, having very little idea of where he was or what he intended to do. He would probably walk until morning until he had no energy left and was utterly spent. Perhaps then he might be able to find a few hours where he could lose himself in sleep and forget how foolish a gentleman he had been.

Breathing heavily, he stopped for a moment, leaning back against a wall, and closed his eyes. Nothing but pain surrounded him.

"And who might you be?" A voice came out to greet him and Felix's eyes snapped open. Turning, he saw only a flickering torch hung from the door of an establishment, which, given the smell emanating from its doors, was not somewhere he wished to be. A man stood in the doorway, a silhouette in the darkness, his voice grating. "I asked you a question."

Shrugging inwardly and thinking it would be best to answer so no argument would be brooked, he shrugged.

"Winterbrook," Felix responded wearily. "And no, I am not coming inside."

As he went to go past the door, a strong arm reached out and grabbed his own.

"This street leads nowhere but here. You'll have to turn around."

Grimacing, Felix let out a frustrated breath, one hand pulling into a fist as the man's hand tightened on his arm.

"I have no business here," he stated firmly, having no intention of permitting himself to become involved in a brawl, even though his temper was already frayed. "I am walking, that is all. I shall turn around and make my way home."

"But nobody comes to these parts unless they want something." The man's voice was low and gravelly, and with a sudden jolt Felix realized that he recognized it. "And I'm sure I know who you are. We've met before. Which means you've been here before."

It was a nervous, brittle laugh that broke from Felix's lips rather than the strong one he had intended as he shook off the man's hand. He *had* been here before, he realized. It was where he had recruited three men to ride with him – one of whom now was standing only inches away.

"I hardly think so. I am from the other side of London. It is not a place where two such fellows like us should meet."

"I'm not so sure about that."

The man reached out for him again, but Felix moved backward quickly. The lantern was the only light, the faded moonlight from behind a cloud hiding most of Felix's features, and for that, he was rather relieved.

"Leave me be."

His anger was rising quickly, fueled by the late evening and the disappointment he had brought upon himself. Recalling that the man had said there was nowhere else to go other than to come back the way he had come, Felix turned quickly but the man stepped in front of him directly. Felix made to sidestep him, but the man moved again, and a sudden fear clawed its way through Felix's anger, settling in his heart.

"I'm sure I know you." The man lowered his head a little as if to scrutinize Felix's face, but Felix quickly turned away. "Your voice. I recognize it."

"And what would you know of upper-class gentlemen?" A fiery response was the only thing he could think to give. Catching a glint of clenched teeth, Felix took his moment and quickly hurried forward. His shoulder crashed against the man's, knocking him backward but, rather than allow

Felix to leave, the man twisted towards him again. Felix had no choice but to defend himself. If this was the man whom he believed it to be, if this was Stafford, then he was just as clumsy on his feet and as heavy in his steps as he had been before. He dodged this way and that as best he could, the cloud moving from the moon to allow him to see a little better. "I have no wish to hurt you!" Felix gasped, staggering back. Stafford made another attempt to lunge for him but this time, Felix knocked him back with one hearty punch. Stafford let out a howl as the crunch of Felix's fist met his cheek, and reeled back from the impact. "I am taking my leave." Breathing hard, Felix stepped forward as Stafford sagged back against the wall. "Leave me alone. We have never met. Do I make myself clear?"

He made turn away only for a dark chuckle to follow after him.

"Now I *know* we have." The man was grinning, laughing aloud as Felix turned around again, his heart twisting painfully. "I knew I recognized your voice and the way that you fought just now? Well, that reminds me of the highwayman I fought a few days ago." Another chuckle came towards him, and Felix shivered. "Which means," Stafford finished, "*you* are that highwayman. And now, *Mr. Winterbrook,* I know your name."

"Think what you wish." Giving the man no firm response to his statement, Felix shrugged and turned around. "And keep your hands off me this time. I have already knocked you back once."

Fighting to keep his steps slow and unhurried, Felix made his way back the way he had come, but he could not help but glance behind him into the shadows, quite certain that he could hear Stafford's dark laughter chasing him. If the man *had* recognized him, if he believed that he *had* found the highwayman, then was there about to be yet more trouble brought to Felix's door? Pausing for a moment, Felix rubbed hard at his forehead, his shoulders sagging, and a heavy sigh escaping from his lungs. He had started off this venture in the hope of finding a little excitement, but now it had brought him nothing but trouble and pain, with the threat of yet more to follow.

CHAPTER THIRTEEN

"I can hardly believe it!" Elizabeth paced up and down the drawing room, as Lady Yardley, Miss Millington, and Lady Sherbourne looked on. "I am now betrothed to a gentleman I have no desire to wed! This goes entirely against the promise I made to myself *and* to my friends. I am horrified at the situation."

Hot tears threatened to push themselves towards her eyes, but with an effort she chased them away, her hands curling into tight fists, her jaw set firmly.

"It is understandable for you to have done so," Miss Millington answered, but Elizabeth dismissed that remark with a wave of her hand.

"No, I ought to have been stronger than that. I should have cared very little for what would occur thereafter. Yes, I acted foolishly, I will admit, in striding into the room to be alone with Lord Winterbrook. It was not the wisest thing to plant a kiss upon Lord Winterbrook's lips, but I had to be sure. I had to know for certain, so that there was no doubt in my own mind."

"And it *was* he who kissed you."

This was said as a statement rather than a question, and Elizabeth nodded, seeing Lady Yardley's sympathetic look.

"Yes, it was he." Stopping her pacing, for her legs were beginning to tremble. Elizabeth made her way back to her chair. "I can hardly believe he has treated me so. I am all the more heartbroken that I am to marry a gentleman who I cannot allow my heart to love."

"Although I do not think that is the way the heart works." Lady Sherbourne offered this remark with a small sigh. "Just because he has made this revelation to you does not mean that your heart will not still desire him. It is a very strange thing, for at this moment there will be a great many sensations, a great sway of emotions at work, including anger, sadness, disappointment, upset, fear, and confusion. Despite this, underneath it all, you may find that your heart is still enamored of him. The affection you had is still within you."

"I can hardly allow myself to believe that." Elizabeth shook her head, unwilling to even think about the fact that she might still be in love with Lord Winterbrook after everything he had done. "That seems to be most peculiar."

"And yet, it is the way of things." Lady Yardley spread out both hands. "And now that you find yourself in this predicament, you must decide what it is you are to do."

Elizabeth nodded, her shoulders dropping, her hands settling in her lap as she looked down at her fingers, which were lacing gently together. She had been dwelling on this for most of the night, and had not allowed herself to consider much else – not even slumber - but now that it was time to face the situation as it stood, her heart was weak with sorrow.

"I do not think that there is very much I *can* do," she answered honestly. "My mother has already written to my father, who will, no doubt, accept Lord Winterbrook's request for my hand. News of the betrothal will be all over London by now, and it *was* I who stepped forward and stated that I was betrothed to Lord Winterbrook. He did permit me to make that choice for myself, and that was what I decided to do at the time."

"But you *do* love him, I suppose, even if you do not wish to." Miss Millington, who had said very little up until this moment, lifted her gaze to Elizabeth. "However, if you decide that you do not wish to marry him, then you could break the betrothal."

Elizabeth sighed.

"I am not certain that I can do so, not after I was the one who stated that we were betrothed. To break it now would cause an uproar! I regret my hastiness, but I fear it is done." The heaviness of that particular statement settled on her shoulders, and she sighed, aware that tears were yet again threatening, but this time making no effort to push them away. "Lord Winterbrook stated that he had an affection for me, said he cared for me, and that his feelings were growing with such significance, his heart was twining itself to mine. But given that he has hidden so much from me, I am not certain that I can believe him."

A short silence spread about the room and Lady Yardley, after some moments of quiet, was the one to break it.

"And that is your fear, is it not?" she asked simply, as Elizabeth swallowed hard and allowed tears to trickle to her cheeks, wiping them away with her handkerchief.

"Yes, that is so." Her vision grew blurry with tears. "I fear it is as Lady Sherbourne says. I fear that my heart is still full of him, although injured by hurt and disappointment. And it is the one thing I do not wish to feel!"

"No one can tell you what to do about Lord Winterbrook. Do not feel that you must stay in your betrothal." Lady Yardley smiled gently. "This must be your own decision."

Tears still seeped from the edges of her eyes.

"I suppose that I should talk to him about all that I feel but, in truth, I have no desire to even see him at the present moment."

"Then you do not need to," Lady Yardley answered firmly. "You must take as much time as you require before you make any further decision. Do not allow pressures from society to push you into a course of action that you might soon regret."

Nodding slowly, Elizabeth managed to dry her tears. It was all still so much of a shock that, at times, she could barely breathe, sensing a great band placed around her chest, squeezing her all the tighter whenever she thought of the highwayman. The highwayman who had stolen her brooch, who had appeared so brash and bold, and who had kissed her without hesitation. She had not seen it before. In all of her considerations, she had never once imagined that Lord Winterbrook could be that man. And yet now that she stood on the other side of it, now that she realized exactly who he was and what he had done, everything seemed to make sense. The boldness, the firmness of character, his twinkling eye, and his bright smile had made her respond in a particular fashion on two separate occasions. That was her shame, she silently admitted, knowing that she had allowed herself to be so completely captured by him. When he had kissed her as the highwayman, he had ignited a spark within her – and that very same spark had roared into life when she had pressed her lips to his. There was no denying it. There was something about him that made her respond in that manner. Was she truly so weak?

Heat billowed through her, and she dropped her head, ashamed that, even now when she thought of him, recalling their kisses, the desire within her remained. The excitement and anticipation still curled within her. How could she think of him in that way, when she knew who he was and what he had done? How could her heart still yearn for him, after what he had taken from her, after what he had hidden from her? It did not make any sense whatsoever.

"I can see this is a strain for you." Speaking quietly, Lady Yardley smiled softly so as not to add any further suffering to Elizabeth's broken heart. "But while he has done to you a great wrong, I would also remind you of the accounts we have heard of this highwayman. In a strange way, Elizabeth, he has done some good, despite the fact that he ought to never have done such a thing in the first place."

Elizabeth sniffed.

"He has helped those in need, I suppose."

"And that came only after he met you, I believe." Miss Millington smiled gently. "You were the person who brought about that change. Once he met you, he no longer took from those he stopped but instead, he did what he could to aid them. If you recall, he has not taken another item from anyone else since he stopped you. That was something he said to you, was it not?"

"He did." Elizabeth lifted both shoulders in a shrug. "But whether or not I can believe him I do not know."

"I suggest that you can in this regard, at least." Spreading out her hands, Lady Yardley's expression remained gentle. "I understand that you will have a great many questions regarding the gentleman but permit yourself to consider the accounts we have been given. Those all speak of the highwayman he *became*. It does not excuse him, as I have said, but he did do some things of great kindness."

Elizabeth nodded but did not really take in what was being said. Her pain was still too great.

"No matter what good he did, he still kept a great deal from me."

"Yes, that is so." Lady Yardley took a deep breath. "It is an unenviable situation, my dear Lady Elizabeth, and I am sorry for it."

"As am I," Miss Millington added. "The secrets he held back from you must now be causing you significant pain."

Swallowing her threatening tears, Elizabeth managed a wan smile.

"I shall find a way." This was said more to herself than to her friends. "Only you three and Lord Winterbrook himself know of my true feelings. For all of society, I shall have to play a part, to pretend that I am satisfied and happy and that all is well between us. Lord Winterbrook will know differently, however."

"Then might I suggest that you speak with him first, *before* you attend a society occasion," Lady Yardley suggested. "Make it plain how you truly feel, so that he will not be deceived by the pretense which you feel required to present to the world. Though I would also encourage you to be as honest as you can with those around you, those you feel close enough to share your heart with. But I understand the pressures which society brings to ladies such as ourselves."

Filling her lungs with air, Elizabeth let the ideas settle in her mind as she let her breath out slowly again. The thought of speaking to Lord Winterbrook was a difficult one, in itself. Even seeing him again was not something she wished for but still, Lady Yardley's advice was wise. It would be best for her to tell Lord Winterbrook precisely what she felt, and to express her concern over their present betrothal. No doubt he would want to give her some explanation for why he had behaved so, but Elizabeth was not sure that she was ready to hear it. In fact, she did not know if she might *ever* be willing to hear it.

"You are going to the ball this evening?"

"Yes. Not that I have any desire to go." Elizabeth spread out her hands. "I do not know if Lord Winterbrook will attend, or if I will have the opportunity to speak with him beforehand. My mother is also attending with me and thus, I cannot refuse or claim that I am unwell, not when she has only just begun to return to society."

Lady Yardley rose from her chair, came towards Elizabeth, and settled a hand on her shoulder, her eyes kind.

"You have a very generous heart, Elizabeth." Her touch was a comfort. "Considerate and generous above all things. I hope that Lord Winterbrook realizes how fortunate he is to have you even willing to step out with him again. I do not think that every lady would do so."

Looking up at Lady Yardley, Elizabeth made to say something, only for a sob to erupt from her throat. Fresh tears came, and before she knew it, she had both hands over her eyes and had broken down completely. Her friends were there to comfort her, and as her tears finally subsided, Elizabeth's resolve grew steady. This was her future she was thinking of and thus, she would have to be entirely truthful with Lord Winterbrook. Whether she could speak with him before the ball or not, she would have to let him know everything her heart felt at present. She would demand to know whether or not he had spoken the truth to her about his affection for her and, if he did not truly care for her, then she would break the betrothal. After all of her resolve, all of her determination, she was not about to let herself fall into the very sort of marriage she had long despised, regardless of what it would do to her standing or her reputation.

I have never allowed myself to even think of marrying a gentleman who cares nothing for me. I will not let Lord Winterbrook steal that hope from me too.

∽

THERE WAS a slight nip in the air, despite it being the height of summer. Some blamed the cold air from the north, but regardless, Elizabeth caught her mother shivering lightly as she stepped out of the carriage.

"Do hurry inside, Mama." Elizabeth gestured to her as she took the arm of the footman, only for her gown to catch on something on the step. Turning, she sought to fix it, glancing over again to see her mother waiting for her. "Mama, please do go. I will only be a moment."

She smiled warmly, and with a nod, her mother stepped away, much to Elizabeth's relief. She certainly could not allow Lady Longford to stay out of doors for too long, not when the air was a little cold. Her gown tugged again and, frustrated, Elizabeth turned to see what the difficulty was. Managing finally to unhook the bottom of her gown from the carriage steps, she was finally free. Inspecting it carefully, for fear it had torn, Elizabeth let out a little breath of relief. Everything was just as it ought to be. Straightening, she smiled and went to hurry into the house, only for a man to step forward directly into her path.

"You're betrothed to Lord Winterbrook."

Elizabeth blinked and took a step back. Her coachman and the carriage had already rolled away, leaving her almost entirely alone. There were one or two footmen nearby somewhere, no doubt waiting for the next carriage to arrive, but for the moment she could not see them.

Her chin lifted as she fought back her fears. The man himself was tall and rather burly, with a state of dress which told her he was not a part of the *ton*. Wherever had he come from?

"Why do you ask?" She did not answer him directly, looking at him steadily, her eyes narrowing. "These are private matters."

"I don't care. I want to know."

The man took a step closer, and Elizabeth instinctively moved back again, fear igniting in her chest.

"I hardly think that this is any of your business. Allow me past."

She kept her words and her voice as firm as she could, but the man only laughed.

"I don't think you understand." Tilting his head, he grinned at her, and Elizabeth shuddered. "Lord Winterbrook owes us."

"Owes you?" Her breath was shuddering out of her, but she remained standing tall, her head held high. "Then what is between you and he means nothing to me. I am no part of it."

"Oh, but you will be," the man answered with a grin. "You see, we had a nice little employment with this Lord Winterbrook of yours. He was paying us to ride with him – nothing more. We hoped he'd give us some of what he stole but he never did. And then we hear he's been giving it all back!" Twisting his head, he spat hard on the ground and Elizabeth could not help but recoil. "Worse still, then he decided he was going to do some good! Instead of doing what a highwayman does, he decided to be noble and didn't even take from the people he stopped! I don't know why he decided to do that, but it didn't please the three of us, I can tell you." Elizabeth said nothing, her eyes darting towards the door and praying that her mother would return, looking for her, wondering where she might have gone. She might run for the door itself, but if she did, then the man could easily grab her, and at the present moment she had very little understanding of what his intentions for her were. "So you're going to tell him that we need him back." The man shrugged. "No one else pays as good as he does."

Elizabeth shuddered.

"You want him to become a highwayman again."

"Yes." The man shrugged, his smile spreading wide again. "It's less of a request but more a demand." Grinning, he laughed darkly. "He's going to come back, he's going to pay us double what he did before, and he's going to start stealing from the people he stops. And *we're* going to get the bounty, not him."

Elizabeth blinked.

"I can promise you, Lord Winterbrook will not agree to any of that."

"Oh yes, he will." The confidence in the man's voice had Elizabeth's heart quailing. "Now we know who he is, and now we know he's betrothed to the likes of you, then we've figured out what it's going to take to get him to do what we want. I don't think it's going to take much guessing on your part either, is it?"

Realizing precisely what he meant, Elizabeth did not allow her whole body to shake with fear as it desired. Instead, she curled her toes in her slippers and folded her fingers into fists to prevent herself from showing any evidence of fear. No doubt he had already guessed that she was very afraid indeed, but she did not want to give the appearance of it.

"Except that I am just about to end our betrothal." Her fingernails dug into her palms. "This may come as a surprise to you, but I am not happy with my betrothal to Lord Winterbrook, and I intend to end it."

The man immediately guffawed, his head thrown back, the sound whirling through the air around her.

"As though I'm about to believe that!" A broad grin had chased away any flicker of hope she had. "You're lying. You're lying so I'll step away from you, but I haven't got a single thought of doing that. You can tell Lord Winterbrook what I've told you. That way he'll know we mean what we say. He might have been able to hide behind his mask for a while, but we know who he is now. There's nowhere for him to hide."

CHAPTER FOURTEEN

Felix was pacing, his thoughts anxious, his stomach twisting. Up and down the hallway he strode outside the ballroom of Lord Gosford's house. It was quite ridiculous to have such anxiety about Lady Elizabeth's arrival, but that was what drove his steps. He ought to be in the ballroom, appearing to be delighted over his betrothal, but instead he was doing nothing but gnawing on the edge of his fingernail and walking up and down the same hallway as he had been doing for the last quarter of an hour.

His attention was caught by a shrill laugh and turning his head, his eyebrows lifted in surprise. The sight of Lady Longford had his heart quickening, but of Lady Elizabeth, however, there was no sign. A gasp caught in his chest. What if she had decided not to attend? His heart turned over at the thought. He could not blame her for such a thing, of course. If she was to remain absent, then he could have no cause to complain. In fact, the only thing he could do was understand. After everything he had done, everything he had hidden from her, it made sense for her to wish to stay away from him.

I must know for certain.

"Lady Longford. How pleasant to see you."

Forcing a bright smile onto his face, he hurried across the hallway, seeing Lady Longford's broad smile as she greeted him. Obviously, Lady Elizabeth had not said a word to her mother about what he had done, and Felix did not know whether to be grateful or humbled.

"Good evening, Lord Winterbrook. How very good it is to see you. Might I say again just how delighted I am over your desire to marry my daughter."

"And I am very grateful that she has accepted me."

These words were spoken with genuine honesty, but at the same time, Felix's tug of guilt pushed away any sense of happiness. The only reason that Lady Elizabeth was marrying him was because she had no other choice than to do so. Had the door not been pushed open by one of the worst gossips in all of London, then their conversation might have taken a very different turn. In all likelihood, their acquaintance would have ended, their close connection severed, and she would have walked out of his life without any further consideration.

"I have received a note from Lord Longford only this morning." Lady Longford smiled warmly and settled a hand on Felix's arm. "He is just as delighted as I."

"I am glad to hear it." Felix inclined his head. "But speaking of Lady Elizabeth, have you any idea of where she might be?"

"She is just behind me, is she not?"

Lady Longford gestured behind her, turning sharply, only to see that Lady Elizabeth was not present. A frown darkened her features and Felix's breath hitched. Whatever had happened to her?

"Lady Longford?"

Lady Longford's face was a little pale.

"She urged me to hurry inside, given that there is slightly cooler air this evening." She began to take some steps back towards the front door of the house. "The bottom of her gown was caught on something, and she did not want me to linger."

"Then wherever could she be?" Felix did not need an answer to this question for, just as they reached the door, Lady Elizabeth stepped through it. Felix's heart leaped with relief, and he went to smile and greet her, only to see the whiteness of her features and her slightly rounded eyes. Something was wrong. "Good evening."

By instinct he reached for her hand, and as her cold fingers went around his, a chill ran over his skin.

"There you are, Elizabeth. I was looking for you." Lady Longford smiled, first at her daughter, and then more warmly, at Felix. "No doubt you will wish to spend a great deal of time with my daughter this evening, Lord Winterbrook. Might you be so kind as to see her into the ballroom?"

"It would be my pleasure." With a quick smile, he released Lady Elizabeth's hand and then offered his arm, which she took quickly. There was no hesitation, no pause, no flicker of her eyes to his. Instead, she simply stood by his side as together, they made their way to the ballroom. "Something has troubled you." Speaking his inner thoughts aloud to her, Felix glanced at his betrothed. "I can tell by your expression that something has happened."

He did not ask whether or not she would be willing to share it with him but had the expectation that she would do so if she wished. If she required help, then he was the one who wanted to offer it to her.

"I have been accosted by a man who claims to know

you." There was a tremble in Lady Elizabeth's frame which Felix felt as her fingers tightened a little on his arm. "He stated that he was in your employ as one of your highwaymen, and that he now desires you to return to that life."

An exclamation catching in his throat, he stopped suddenly as she turned to face him.

"Where did he speak with you?"

His voice was low and urgent, and Lady Elizabeth closed her eyes briefly, her face pale.

"Outside." Licking her lips, she shook her head. "I do not know how he recognized me but, evidently, he was waiting for my arrival. I cannot understand how he knows who I am, in connection to you."

"Because I, in my foolishness, gave him my name." Frustrated with himself for not only having spoken his own name to Stafford when he had been aimlessly wandering through London, he now realized just how much danger that had put Lady Elizabeth in. With her connection to him, he could not easily keep her safe from the three men he had ridden with previously. "What did this man want?"

Lady Elizabeth took another moment, obviously still shaken by her experience.

"He wanted me to tell you that their expectation is for you to return to your highwayman disguise." She took a moment, looking away from him, one hand at her throat. "And that they expect you to pay them as you have done before with an increase on top of that. From what he said, I believe he also expects you to steal from those you stop and that what you take from them will then be shared out amongst the three of them equally."

Angry at such demands, Felix shook his head, his free hand balling into a fist.

"I will not do so."

"He also said that if you did refuse, there would be consequences." Lady Elizabeth's voice had dropped significantly until it was just above a whisper. "I stated that I was to end our betrothal this very evening but that made very little difference. He did not believe me, and certainly will still use my connection to you regardless."

A hole tore itself in Felix's heart.

"You intended to end our betrothal this evening?"

"I was not certain what I intended," she answered, hoarsely. "I wanted to speak with you privately before this ball. I wanted to spend time explaining my present situation, my thoughts, and my feelings, but that has been snatched from me by this man's arrival."

Felix swallowed.

"Then why did you say such a thing?"

"In the hope that he would leave me alone... but it was no use."

Wishing he could sweep her into his arms, Felix closed his eyes for a moment, waiting to see if a moment of clarity would come to him, an immediate answer which might help him know what to do - but nothing came.

"Come." Without being able to linger out in the hallway any longer, he had no choice but to lead Lady Elizabeth into the ballroom. She accepted his arm and, as they walked together into the room which was crowded with the rest of the guests, the hubbub of laughter and music was overwhelming; a distorted fanfare to his tormented thoughts. "I should never have suggested courtship." Muttering darkly, Felix pushed one hand through his hair, looking back when Lady Elizabeth caught her breath. "That is not to say that I had no wish to, Lady Elizabeth – pray do not misunderstand me. My desire to court you was very strong indeed, just as it is now. However, I fear that my foolishness has now brought you into danger and it is *that* which I regret."

Lady Elizabeth sniffed, and to his horror, a single tear ran down her cheek.

"But that does not solve our situation at present, Lord Winterbrook."

His smile was a little stiff.

"No, it does not."

What answer could he give her? What solution could he offer her? Nothing came to mind.

"Who is the man? Is it all as he says?" Lady Elizabeth sniffed and looked away. "Is he indeed a man you paid to ride with you?"

Wishing that the floor would open up to swallow him whole, Felix had no choice but to nod.

"It will either be Stafford, Griggs, or Connolly." He could not hide anything from her now. "These are three men I hired to ride with me in my activities as a highwayman. I did not think about how foolish such an action was until much later. I made it clear from the beginning that I would always return whatever I took, as the enjoyment for me was simply the thrill of chasing the carriage, having it stop at my command, and playing the part of a highwayman. It was a disguise that offered me a different life for a time." It all sounded so very weak and, wincing, Felix looked away from her. "I should have expected that these men would do something akin to this. I had never revealed to them my name nor shown them my face, but they have recently discovered it – again, thanks to my own foolishness. No doubt they will have been able to learn of our betrothal through various questions of people who work as servants of the *ton*'s gossips. I cannot tell you how sorry I am that they have involved you."

Lady Elizabeth's lips trembled, but when she spoke, her voice was steady.

"So they wish you to return to that situation so that they earn more than they have previously."

"Yes, it seems so." Felix ran one hand over his eyes, his jaw tense, his whole body tightening with frustration. "For the moment, I find myself greatly perturbed. These men are the very worst sort of ruffians. The reason I dispersed them, in the end, was because they attempted to force me into stealing from Lord Stanfield when I stated that I would not. It seems now that they are determined to do whatever they can to force my hand – which includes threatening you."

Groaning, he allowed his anger to grow, though his shame grew with it.

"Then what can be done?"

Lady Elizabeth's wide eyes begged him for an answer, but Felix had none. The only thing he could suggest, he rebelled against inwardly. The silence grew between them and, as she continued to look to him for an answer, it was the only thing he could offer her. His heart tore itself into pieces and it took him some moments to force the words from his lips. All they brought with them was pain.

"You should end your connection to me. You should end it at once."

Lady Elizabeth's eyes flared as they stood together at the edge of the ballroom, one hand going to her mouth.

"Whatever do you mean?"

"I mean you should not marry me. You should make certain that all of society knows our connection is at an end. Perhaps that will be enough to convince these men that you are of no importance to me, even though it is precisely the *opposite* of what I desire."

Rather than immediately agree, Lady Elizabeth

frowned, her lips pulled tight as she dropped her gaze to the floor. Felix held his breath, certain that she would agree at any moment, only for her to shake her head.

"I do not particularly like being forced into any action. Lord Winterbrook." Her eyes lifted suddenly to his. "Nor do I like being told what I must do."

"I am only attempting to keep you safe."

"I have something I must ask you." Changing the subject entirely, Lady Elizabeth took a step closer to him, her hand finding his. Her fingers did not lace through his but gripped his hand tightly, as though they were two gentlemen making the most severe of handshakes. "Tell me if you truly meant everything you have said to me."

Not quite certain what she meant, Felix frowned.

"What do you mean? In what I have professed to you?" Lady Elizabeth gave only the smallest nod, her eyes holding his, and Felix's heart lurched. "I have never once told you a mistruth. I have not shared things with you, certainly, although there was at least one time when I considered telling you about my highwayman disguise." Sighing, he pressed her fingers. "I can promise you that every word I have spoken to you about my heart and my affections has been entirely true." Lady Elizabeth blinked rapidly, and her eyes suddenly became glassy, though she did not look away. Felix's heart began to pound furiously as if somehow it realized that these next few moments would be of the greatest significance. "I have only ever told you the truth about my affections.". Speaking quietly, he took a small step closer, feeling the urge to repeat what he had said. "My heart thinks only of you."

Nodding, Lady Elizabeth's tongue darted out to moisten her lips.

"Then do you mean to say that you still care for me?"

"I do." He pressed his free hand against his heart. "You cannot know how much it tears me asunder to know that I have injured you so severely. I never wanted you to find out about my highwayman disguise and certainly not in the way that you did. I wished it to be entirely in the past. There will be time to explain it, time for me to talk with you about all that I have done if you still wish, but I can assure you, Elizabeth, my heart has been yours from the very first moment that we met."

A tiny smile edged up the corner of her mouth.

"Truly?"

"Truly." A little emboldened, he smiled back at her. "I could not help but kiss you that day. It was bold and uncouth, and certainly not something I ought to have done, but I was in my guise as a highwayman and therefore, I acted upon my desire. I am certain that in doing so, it was in that moment that our hearts melded."

From the look in her eyes, it appeared as though Lady Elizabeth did not know what to say. She was somewhere between weeping and smiling, but she gave no response other than to look away. Perhaps she was confused and uncertain over all that he had said, and Felix could not blame her for that. It had been two days since their previous conversation, and they had not yet had the opportunity to speak about what had taken place – and now yet further difficulty had come upon them. Little wonder then, that she did not know how to respond to him.

"But I must find a way to extricate you from the situation," he said softly. "You must end our betrothal - it is the only way."

Lady Elizabeth took a deep breath, lifting her gaze back to his. With another breath, she lifted her chin and looked him straight in the eye.

"No."

Felix reared back at her response, overcome with both surprise and relief.

"No? But after what I have done and after the situation you are now in, surely you can see –"

"I believe that your words of affection are genuine, at least." Lady Elizabeth interrupted him, color beginning to return to her face. "I will not be chased away from something, simply because three men have decided that I will be a pawn for them to place where they will."

Felix ran one hand through his hair, fear of what might become of her beginning to twist through him.

"You put yourself in danger by remaining with me."

"I am already in danger." So saying, she shrugged lightly. "I believe I will be just as much in danger in the future as I am at present, should we end our connection. These gentlemen know that I am betrothed to you, and regardless of whether or not it truly does stand between us, they will still pursue me. They intend to force your hand, heedless of who they hurt in the process. They believe that I am of some significance to you, and will not care whether our betrothal stands or not. Do you not see it? There is a difficulty here and it must be solved in another way."

"But how can we do so?" Felix did not see an easy way out. "I must do as they ask. I will not have you injured, not in any way."

"And I appreciate that." For a moment, Lady Elizabeth's lips curved, but then the smile fell away. "They are determined to have you ride with them again. If you do not, then they will no doubt expose you to all of London. Your reputation will be ruined and my name along with it."

"I had not considered that." Ashamed of his own selfishness, Felix dropped his head and closed his eyes tightly. "I cannot permit you to do this. You must step away from me."

He opened his eyes just as Lady Elizabeth tossed her head, letting her gaze fly around the ballroom.

"I am sure that there is many a gentleman present who has done far worse than you," she stated clearly. "That is not to say that I condone what you have done, nor the reasons behind it, but at the very least, you made amends. You returned what you took, and you appeared to be doing all you could to aid those you stopped. I know that one betrothal was brought to an end - not before time, I hear - and I assume Miss Whitford and her granduncle were also your doing?"

A tight laugh came to Felix's lips. He tried to push it away, but it came out, nonetheless.

"I could not think of where else to send them." Looking away, embarrassed, he tried to explain. "I told them to go and seek out Lord Winterbrook or Lord Bramwell for what else could I do? I knew that I was taking a risk in revealing to them that I was someone who knew people of the highest echelons of society, but I could not permit them to continue on to their intended lodgings, not when I knew what would happen to Miss Whitford if they did so. Besides which, I know Miss Whitford's stepbrother, and was all the more angry at his behavior. How could I not step in? How could I not find a safer place for them to reside? I could not allow Miss Whitford to go to the East End, as her granduncle planned. She might have lost everything of value to her and her granduncle could have lost his own life! No, I could not let that remain on my conscience, not when I could do something about it, and thus, I told them to make their way to my townhouse." There was a short silence and Felix winced inwardly, realizing that he had spoken rather fervently. He had not meant to permit his emotions such sway but, recalling how Miss Whitford and her granduncle had been when he had first stopped them, his feelings had come to the fore. "I am only glad that Lord Bramwell is to marry her. Such news has made me very happy indeed."

Lady Elizabeth smiled. Her eyes lit with a gentle flame, and for the first time, Felix's own heart rose. He had been desperate for her to smile at him again, though he had not realized it until this moment. How beautiful she was! How much he desired her company, how much he wished to make amends to her, in any way that he could.

"All of this is why I say that there are many other gentlemen who have done far worse than you." Her smile lingered. "I speak to myself also, I think. I see now that there is some goodness in your actions. You have given Miss Whitford a happy future. You have protected her granduncle and you have done many other things to aid and support those who needed it. I should not like your reputation to be ruined, not when you have done some good. It is better than being a scoundrel through and through, is it not?" Felix could not account for her kindness. What could he say to her in response? He could not accept her words that he was no better or worse than any other gentleman, feeling the weight of his guilt settle upon him all the heavier, as though her words had added to his shame. "Because of this, I will not let these men ruin you or end our betrothal. Any decisions on these matters will be of my own mind and of my own considerations." The determination in her tone made him smile briefly. She had returned to her usual self, her confidence and poise filling him with admiration. "We shall find a way."

Felix held out one hand and after a moment. Lady Elizabeth took it. He bent forward over it, his lips to the back of her hand, lingering there as he squeezed his eyes closed and allowed his heart to settle into a calmer rhythm. He had been so afraid. Afraid that he would lose her, afraid that his life and his future, as he had hoped, would be quite ruined, and all by his own doing. Now, however, Lady Elizabeth was giving him a further opportunity - one he did not deserve, and one he certainly did not want to lose. There was still the chance that she might decide to break off their betrothal regardless, but at least she would not do so because of blackmail, or out of fear. He could not help but admire her for that.

"We must ask Lady Yardley, Lady Sherbourne, and Miss Millington for their advice." Lady Elizabeth squeezed his fingers gently as he lifted his head. "What say you, Lord Winterbrook, will you allow us to discuss the matter? To find a way forward together?"

"I will do whatever I must."

He did not have any pride left within him, no desire to face this future on his own. In this, he was more than contented, more than willing to accept whatever help he could be offered - even if it meant availing himself to these ladies. If it meant baring his heart and revealing his foolishness to them all, he would do it. He would do anything to keep Lady Elizabeth safe.

"Then shall we take tea tomorrow?" The gentleness of her smile burned into him, searing his heart all over again. "It will be at Lady Yardley's, I think. I will make the arrangements."

Swallowing at the tightness in his throat, Felix simply gazed upon her for a long moment.

"You are without comparison, Lady Elizabeth." Taking a breath, he inclined his head to her, lost in her goodness. "I can do nothing but thank you."

Her smile grew soft.

"Shall we dance, Lord Winterbrook?"

A little overwhelmed, Felix stepped back, staring at her as if she had quite lost her senses.

"You wish to dance? With me?"

Lady Elizabeth offered him a small smile.

"I do recall that we enjoy dancing the waltz together, do we not?"

Felix could not bring himself to speak. The sweetness of Lady Elizabeth, the generosity of her heart, after all that he had done, was more than he deserved. Saying nothing, he bowed towards her, then offered her his arm.

"Thank you, Lord, Winterbrook."

"Are you certain that you wish to waltz with me?"

Hearing the gruffness in his voice, aware that it betrayed his emotions, Felix gazed at his betrothed with a steadiness he did not feel within him. Searching her face, eager to know if she truly was doing so because she desired it or only because she felt the need to keep up the pretense of happiness and contentment for those who would be watching.

"I do enjoy the waltz." came her gentle reply. "And I enjoy it the most when I am dancing it with you."

Her eyes averted, but a slight pink rose in her cheeks as Felix found himself grinning broadly. Feeling as though he had been offered the greatest gift a gentleman had ever been presented with, he walked steadily, with Lady Elizabeth on his arm, towards the center of the room. As he walked, Felix made a silent promise to himself: no matter how much it took from him, he would do whatever was required to make amends. His only aim now was to heal the wound he had left upon Lady Elizabeth's heart.

CHAPTER FIFTEEN

*E*lizabeth looked across the room. Thus far, everyone sat in silence, and she felt the growing tension to be almost insurmountable. From the look on Miss Millington's face, it was quite clear that she was not particularly enamored of Lord Winterbrook's presence, and Elizabeth could not blame her for feeling so. Lord Winterbrook had not exactly behaved well, but when they had spoken the previous evening, something within her had shifted. It was difficult to explain, and difficult to understand precisely what it was, but she recognized it, nonetheless. It was just as Lady Sherbourne had suggested. Under all of the pain and upset that Lord Winterbrook had brought, the affection for him was something she had been unable to remove from her heart.

In the carriage on the way to the ball, the decision about whether to continue with their betrothal or to end it had been swirling in her mind. She had reminded herself that it would rely solely on whether or not Lord Winterbrook's supposed affection for her had been genuine and in that, he had proven himself. It had come when they had been talking about her altercation with Stafford, when Lord Winterbrook himself had insisted that she end their betrothal for her sake.

It was then that she had realized the truth, had seen the suffering in his eyes, and had believed that his words had been honest. Everything he had said to her regarding his own feelings, she did not doubt any longer. He had been a gentleman altered, one she did not recognize, for he had been almost distraught over what Stafford had done. When she had spoken of the threats, Lord Winterbrook's expression had been wild and furious in equal measure, afraid for her, ashamed of what he had done, and what his behavior had brought about. Despite what it would do to his own heart, he had been desperate to protect her and, in seeing that, Elizabeth had come to realize that what she had longed for, what she had long dreamed of, and what she had promised herself was still within her grasp. It did not mean that their connection was entirely secure, nor that she was perfectly happy, or entirely able to forgive him, but there was still hope. Hope that she might still have a marriage of love rather than of convenience. Much was still to be healed but for the most part, she was willing to give their connection another opportunity to thrive. This meant that, for the moment, they would have to face a most difficult situation with these three men who were determined to have Lord Winterbrook return to their way of life.

"My apologies." Lady Yardley sailed into the room and immediately the sharp tension broke. Elizabeth smiled quickly as Lord Winterbrook rose to his feet, but Lady Yardley waved one hand. "No need for formality I assure you. I can see that tea has already been served." She offered a quick smile to Lady Sherbourne. "Thank you, my dear.

The situation is at present rather difficult, I understand, Lord Winterbrook?"

Lord Winterbrook cleared his throat. His face was a little red as he spoke, but he said every word clearly and distinctly.

"Yes. It is all my own fault, I confess. I was foolish in what I did, for I never once considered that there would be such severe consequences, not only for myself, but also for Lady Elizabeth. I never intended for her to become involved in such a way and now that she has been threatened, I am greatly tormented."

He continued his explanation, holding nothing back and sharing everything which had happened.

Anyone who listened would have no other choice but to believe him, such was the sincerity of his words. Elizabeth watched as Miss Millington's eyebrows lifted. Her gaze turned towards Elizabeth, who then nodded as if to confirm that all he had said was true.

"And that is the state of things, as they stand." Lord Winterbrook finished with a heavy sigh, then gestured to Elizabeth with one hand. "I can only finish by saying how sorrowful I am that Lady Elizabeth was involved in this matter. I did not ever think that such a thing would happen, but then again, I did not consider things carefully. I only considered myself and my desire to be a little entertained. Desires which have proven themselves to be more than a little ridiculous."

Lady Yardley sighed heavily.

"It is a troubling situation." Her eyes alighted upon Elizabeth. "That must have been very trying for you also, Lady Elizabeth. I can imagine it would have been a rather terrifying experience."

Elizabeth nodded.

"It was," she admitted, refusing to even permit herself to say anything other than the truth, having no desire to pretend that she had evidenced a good deal more bravery. "I did attempt to speak firmly, but the man was all too aware of how much power he had. My fear was obvious to him, I think."

"You cannot know the depth of my regret in this matter." Lord Winterbrook dropped his head forward this time, not looking at anyone as he spoke. "I did ask Lady Elizabeth to end our betrothal so that she might be free from this, so that she would be protected, but she has not accepted my suggestion."

With his head lifting, he looked at her again, but she simply shook her head as well to confirm that no, she would not be ending their connection. Three pairs of eyes turned towards her. Lady Yardley, Miss Millington, and Lady Sherbourne all looked at her, questions written on every face.

"I would not allow myself to be so intimidated." Understanding their silent questions, Elizabeth gave them her answers. "If I am to end the betrothal, then I will do it on my terms rather than on anyone else's."

This explanation had Lady Yardley smiling, though Elizabeth blushed a little.

"You have always been quietly determined, Lady Elizabeth."

"Which I think is a very good quality." Lord Winterbrook murmured, his eyes still haunted as he gazed back across the room toward Elizabeth. "Though perhaps in this, I would have preferred you not to be so!"

Elizabeth managed a smile, the edge of which touched Lord Winterbrook's lips also.

"I do have an idea as to how this might be resolved, however." She had not slept much the previous night, having had too many thoughts of Lord Winterbrook and his difficulties filling her mind. Slowly she was able to untangle the threads until a solution had presented itself. "From my perspective, it seems as though we only have two choices. The first is to refuse these men and thereafter, to see just how far they will go to bring Lord Winterbrook back to them. If they are honest, they do not wish to reveal him to society, even though they have threatened to do as much. They will lose the money he paid them - the wages they desire to have again."

Lord Winterbrook nodded slowly.

"That is true."

"It does not mean that they will not do what they must to force you," Elizabeth continued with a wry smile. "And given that I do not want to put myself in any particular danger, there is a second option also."

"Which is?"

"Which is to unmask these men instead." Smiling, she tilted her head. "We must set up a scene where they believe that they are in charge, and that you are doing as they ask. However, at the end of it, they will be caught, and you will find yourself free of these men. They will be unwilling and unable to come after you, and instead, they themselves will be in fear of what consequences might fall upon them."

Lord Winterbrook blinked slowly, then shook his head.

"If this is to put you in yet more danger then I do not want you to do anything at all," he said firmly, only for Elizabeth to swipe the air with her hand, cutting him off.

"And I have already said that I am determined to see this through. I will not have anyone using me to blackmail you. *This* is a way in which we can force these men to reconsider, to have them see that their plan was not as well thought out as they believed it to be. Trust me, Lord Winterbrook, you *will* be free from this."

"But I do not deserve it." His voice and his words were so quiet, Elizabeth leaned forward in her chair, as though it might help her to catch them. "I am a gentleman who has almost ruined himself, and for no other reason apart from my selfishness. I do not deserve such kindness."

"And yet you have it." Lady Yardley spoke briskly. "There is no need for self-pity, Lord Winterbrook. Instead, I suggest that you consider how grateful you are that Lady Elizabeth is not only standing by you but willing to aid you in this manner."

A slight hint of color came into Lord Winterbrook's face, but rather than respond, he merely nodded. He did not smile but simply looked at her, and as Elizabeth held his gaze, she felt her heart begin to sing. There was a connection between them still, a connection she could not deny. She did not want to end this betrothal. Yes, she had always promised herself that she would marry a gentleman who loved her, and she had no doubts now that Lord Winterbrook was the man to do so. The truth was that he loved her in the same way that she loved him, even though those particular words had not been spoken as yet. But from his actions, from his words and from his expressions, she knew it was so. It seemed that Lady Sherbourne had been correct to state that her heart would still be full of him, regardless of what he had done, and in a way, Elizabeth was glad of it. If they were to work through this present difficulty, to work through his secrets, perhaps it would make their connection even stronger. Yes, it would take time, but she trusted that he would not keep such things from her again. There was still hope, and hope she would allow herself to cling to.

"Tell us of your plan." Miss Millington reached forward to take her teacup. "I will help you in whatever way I can."

"I thank you, my dear friend."

With a broad smile, Elizabeth sat forward and then began to outline what she intended, as she watched every face begin to enliven with interest. By the time she was finished, even Lord Winterbrook was almost smiling.

"Remarkable." Lord Winterbrook threw up his hands as she finished. "Absolutely remarkable. I find myself amazed by your wisdom."

"As do I!" Lady Yardley agreed, laughing. "Now when do you plan to do this? When shall it take place?"

Elizabeth lifted an eyebrow in Lord Winterbrook's direction.

"Shall we say in two days' time? Will that give you enough opportunity to speak to Stafford?"

Lord Winterbrook rolled his eyes.

"It will be *more* than enough time. I assure you. They will be ready to ride the moment I speak with them!" Taking a deep breath, he put his hands out. "But I think this is the best plan. I can think of nothing else. I thank you, Lady Elizabeth, for your wisdom and your willingness."

"I look forward to this matter being behind us."

She spoke fervently, praying that he would understand her meaning and, from the smile which split his face and the light which gleamed in his eyes, she believed he did. This would be the end of the dark situation which had wrapped itself around them, and in its place, would leave nothing but a glorious light.

"How do you feel?"

Elizabeth looked down at her tightened hands, her fingers white with tension.

"I am very anxious." She attempted a laugh, but it was a brittle sound, and one which was chased away very quickly. "This may very well have been my own idea, but I confess to being very nervous. I do hope that the outcome will be as we expect."

Lady Yardley nodded but said nothing. She too was looking less poised than usual, although her expression appeared calm. It was the slight paleness of her face, and how her eyes darted around the carriage which gave Elizabeth the impression that she was also a little uncertain of what was going to take place.

"I am sure that all will go very well." Miss Millington stated this with a great amount of confidence in her voice, but she too was looking white-faced. Lord Yardley sat opposite his wife for when Lady Yardley had informed him of what was to happen, he had not just volunteered to join them but had insisted. He was not about to let his wife, or her friends, sit in a carriage that was about to be robbed by highwaymen without him being present. Elizabeth had widened her eyes at the sight of a pistol being placed upon the seat, with Lord Yardley hiding it with his coat, but he, upon seeing her reaction, had assured her that it was only there as a precaution. Elizabeth had nodded, still uncertain, but now found herself silently grateful for the knowledge that they were protected.

"Wrap your scarf a little higher about your neck." Lady Yardley reached across, tapping Elizabeth's knee to garner her attention. "And pull the bonnet a little lower, if you can. Recall, we do not want you to be identified."

Elizabeth did as she was told, hiding her features as best she could, knowing that when the time came, she would have to round her back and pull her shoulder high in an attempt to appear somewhat infirm. Lord Winterbrook had stated that he hoped very much that *he* would be the one to stop the carriage and demand that they gave him what they had, but he could not be certain of it. If Stafford, Connelly, or Griggs came forward, then they would have to make certain that Elizabeth could not be recognized by any of them. Lord Winterbrook had suggested that she remain in London, but Elizabeth had refused. Her friends were to be a part of this, and so, therefore, was she. The thought of sitting alone at home while Miss Millington, Lord Yardley, and Lady Yardley put themselves in a dangerous situation was unconscionable. Thus, she sat and waited for the result of whatever this afternoon would bring, closing her eyes and taking in a breath to quieten her fractious mind.

All the same, she jumped in fright when a loud shout rent the air. There was more than one voice this time, each shouting and, even though she knew precisely who it was, and what they intended, she shuddered violently. The coachman, who had been prepared in advance for this, slowed the horses carefully and did not make a single sound of contention. There was laughter and much shouting from the highwaymen and, when the door was pulled open, Elizabeth shrank back, her heart pounding furiously.

"Step out. All of you."

It was not Lord Winterbrook who stood there, as Elizabeth had hoped, but rather the man who had confronted her a few days ago, Stafford. She could tell by his frame, the heaviness of him, the broadness of his shoulders. His gruff voice sent a tremor through her, and she hastily dropped her chin and rounded her back as best she could, looking away from him to hide her face.

"We will not." Lord Yardley gestured towards Elizabeth. "I will not drag this poor lady from her chair. We must get her to London." His voice was flooded with anger. "And besides, I am not usually at the behest of highwaymen."

"Well, today you are," Stafford retorted, grimly. "I insist that all of you remove yourselves from the carriage. Either you help her, or I will drag her out myself."

There was another frank exchange, but after a few moments, Lord Yardley yielded. Turning his head, he murmured for them to do as was asked, and then stepped out first. Lady Yardley went next, with Miss Millington, thereafter, leaving Elizabeth to hobble forward. Carefully, she made her way from the carriage, pretending to be bent and twisted and leaning heavily on Lord Yardley's arm. When she stood on the grass, Elizabeth leaned heavily against the side of the carriage, turning to one side so that the men would not see her face fully. Stafford was standing directly in front of them all, another man to his left. A third man was near the coachman, his pistol drawn and pointed in the fellow's direction.

"Give us whatever you have." Stafford waved one hand to the other man. "Go to the luggage."

Another man, a wiry figure, made to step forward, only for Lord Yardley to speak up.

"I would take a moment to reconsider, if I were you."

Out of the corner of her eye, Elizabeth watched, surprised. The man who had begun to make his way to the carriage stopped at once, as though Lord Yardley was the one to give him his orders, rather than Stafford. Glancing quickly to her right, she saw Lord Winterbrook sitting astride his horse, the only one still to do so. Perhaps he had not been given permission by Stafford to jump to the ground. He was not looking at her, but her heart went out to him regardless. Hastily, Elizabeth pulled her eyes away, fearful that someone would notice her lingering glance. It was not time yet for her to reveal herself, but it soon would be. She could not allow that moment to come too quickly.

"What are you doing?" Stafford waved one hand at the other man. "Hurry up. Work through that luggage as quickly as you can."

The man glanced at Lord Yardley and then took another step, only for Lady Yardley to speak again.

"I think he shows some wisdom in being cautious." Her words came clearly, and though Stafford took a slow step towards her, she did not flinch. "I would advise you to do the same. It is important that you listen to me at present."

"Is that so? Or is it that you have things you are trying to hide from me?" Stafford snorted, gesturing to the second man who again, made his way towards the carriage, coming to a stop beside Elizabeth, his eyes glinting as he studied her – no doubt wondering what jewels she might be hiding. "Do you think that your words will stop me from doing what I want? You should know better than that by now! I am sure you've heard stories of highwaymen." Lowering his head and his tone, he grinned wickedly. "We are just as cruel as you might believe."

"And just as foolish." Miss Millington spoke clearly, even though she trembled as she did so. "You have very little idea of who it is you are speaking to."

Elizabeth's eyes flared as Stafford's expression grew ugly. His jaw pushed forward, his brow lined heavily as he took slow advancing steps towards Miss Millington, while the second man stepped back from Elizabeth, glaring at Miss Millington for daring to say such a thing.

"I don't care who I am speaking to," Stafford growled, his eyes dark. "Be it rich or poor, they will *all* give me something. I don't care whether you serve the King himself, or if you have no home but the street. Whatever you have, I will take it."

"Then it shall be the last thing you do take," Lord Yardley stated, coming to stand in front of Miss Millington as though to protect her from Stafford. "You have been given an opportunity, but if you refuse to take it, then there is nothing I can do other than to tell you all that this shall be the last time you will ever attempt to rob someone."

Rather than respond angrily, Stafford merely laughed. It was the same cold, cruel laugh that Elizabeth had heard when he had spoken to her alone, and it still sent a chill over her skin.

"I hardly think so."

Lady Yardley sniffed.

"Perhaps you might reconsider once I tell you that I write 'The London Ledger'."

At this, Stafford merely rolled his eyes.

"Do you really think that people like me have heard something like that?" He laughed again. "I don't get to reading much."

"Then allow me to explain to you what it is." Again, Lady Yardley spoke calmly, but Elizabeth's heart quickened, knowing that this was the moment when the truth would be revealed. "I write it myself. It is full of tidbits and pieces of information which the *ton* all pay great attention to. Names, descriptions... all of those are kept within it. I am certain that they would be very pleased indeed to know that I have a full description of the men who robbed us."

Elizabeth held her breath, heat building as she watched for Stafford's reaction. The man did precisely what she had expected and, after a moment, threw back his head and roared with laughter. Lady Yardley did not flinch, however. She simply looked at him, waiting, a tiny smile flickering across her lips. When Stafford had finally recovered himself - with both of his other men laughing too, he threw up his hands and grinned at Lady Yardley.

"And what would you say?" he asked, still chuckling. "Would you say that I am a tall, broad-shouldered man, that this fellow here is a little smaller, and that this man here is the skinniest you have ever seen?." Another laugh followed this, and his eyes were still dark but dancing with obvious merriment. "I hardly think such descriptions will be enough for the gentlemen of London to come in pursuit of us."

"It might." Lady Yardley shrugged. "Although it would be even better if I had your names."

Stafford gestured to both of his men.

"You talk nonsense."

As the man who had been sent to the luggage began to move closer to Elizabeth again, she could not prevent herself from shuddering furiously. Looking at her friend, she caught the small smile on Lady Yardley's face and knew that the time was upon them.

"Yes, indeed, it would be a good deal easier if I could have your names," Lady Yardley said again, speaking more loudly than before, and, with a breath, Elizabeth stepped forward. Turning sharply, she pointed one finger towards Stafford.

"That man is Stafford," she said clearly, seeing the man's confident smile vanish. "And his two companions are Connelly and Griggs. They are men who linger in the East End of London in an establishment named 'The Tawdry Pony'. I think all of those details, Lady Yardley, would be of particular interest to the *ton*. I am certain that there are those who would immediately go in search of these men, given that they now have their names and their descriptions and information about where they like to reside, also."

As she spoke, Lord Winterbrook dismounted from his horse. He moved slowly, but Elizabeth did not give him even the slightest attention, only catching his movements from the corner of her eye. The three men were now staring at her, with the man by the coachman slowly beginning to come towards Stafford, his face a little pale. Stafford did not smile. In fact, he was staring at her with such wide eyes that she feared they might fall from his head if he continued much longer.

"I think it would be a very fair description indeed," Lady Yardley murmured quietly. "And as I have said, 'The London Ledger' is read by almost every gentleman and lady in the upper echelons of society. They have a great deal of power when they act together, and I can assure you that they will put everything they have into finding you and ending your... endeavors here."

"It's you!" Stafford's voice was low and filled with fury as he turned his face in Elizabeth's direction. "It's Lady Elizabeth, isn't it?"

As Stafford began to stride forward, Elizabeth went to move back, only for Lord Winterbrook to act.

Stafford, being entirely unprepared, was jerked backward as Lord Winterbrook took hold of him from behind. His pistol was in his other hand and, as he lifted it, the atmosphere darkened instantly. Having been knocked off his feet, Stafford stopped still for a moment. With a scowl, he attempted to slowly rise, his hands lifting a little as he swung slowly around.

"So you think that you can threaten us?" Stafford's tone was dark as Lord Yardley gestured for the man near her - Connelly or Griggs, Elizabeth did not know which - to make his way back towards the horses next to Stafford.

Quite when he had taken his pistol from his coat, Elizabeth did not know, but she was grateful that he had.

"And you can come here also." With a chuckle, Lord Yardley gestured for the third man to join his friends. "There will be no stealing from us today. And if you think to attempt anything, let me tell you that the article for 'The London Ledger' is already written, and is in the safe hands of my staff. Should anything happen to prevent us from returning, it will be published."

The three men stood before them but, with a smirk, Stafford chuckled.

"You really believe that you've succeeded." Stafford laughed again, though Elizabeth could not understand why, given the fact that he was clearly at a disadvantage. "You say that you'll write our names and our descriptions in 'The London Ledger', but what is to stop us from naming Lord Winterbrook also?"

Elizabeth strode forward, no longer afraid, her confidence billowing as she faced up to Stafford.

"And who do you think the *ton* will believe?" Tilting her head, her hands going to her hips, she arched an eyebrow. "Do you think that any of them will accept the idea that three rogues such as yourselves can be trusted?"

"And when do you expect to speak to any gentlemen who come in search of you?" Miss Millington added, her voice still trembling but her confidence growing as she came to stand beside Elizabeth. "Do you intend to tell them about Lord Winterbrook before or after they shoot you?"

At her words, Stafford's face blanched, his confident smile shattering. There was nowhere for them to go, no route they might take to escape, and gain the upper hand. They might very well attempt to blame Lord Winterbrook, but Elizabeth was confident that none in the *ton* would believe them. Miss Millington was right - it was not as though any of these three men would have the opportunity to speak of it.

"Might I suggest that you take this opportunity to ride away and never return to your endeavors here?" Lord Winterbrook spoke loudly, his pistol pressing into Stafford's back. "You will not threaten me. You will not threaten Lady Elizabeth. You will not threaten any one of us, ever again. You will not ride and pursue carriages any longer."

There was a trace of anger in his voice, but he remained steady as Elizabeth pressed one hand to her stomach, praying that Stafford, Griggs, and Connelly would see the sense in what they were being offered.

"This is your only opportunity," Lord Yardley added. "If you do not take it now, then we will take you into London ourselves and tell those closest to the King precisely who you are and what you have been doing."

"You are one of us!" Griggs spat, twisting around angrily to face Lord Winterbrook, but Lord Winterbrook only laughed.

Ripping the mask from his face, he threw it to the ground.

"I do not know what you mean!" he exclaimed. "I was riding in the carriage with my friends and my betrothed when we were set upon by three highwaymen." The smile fled as he scowled. "So either you ride away from us and never threaten us again, or you will bring the consequences upon yourselves."

A few minutes later, Elizabeth's eyes followed the three men riding away from the carriage, in the opposite direction from London. Lord Yardley had taken their pistols and Lord Winterbrook had demanded their masks. They had given them to him reluctantly, but there had been no other choice but for them to do as he instructed. He had been close to taking the horses as well but had permitted them to keep them. Elizabeth was sure that they would keep their word, for the moment at least although, no doubt, they would soon return to the city in search of other ways to do whatever evil they wished. For her, however, the darkness was gone.

Lord Winterbrook came towards her, his face free of all worry and care.

"It seems as though your plan has succeeded." Taking her hand, he lifted it to his lips, bending his head forward. "And I am forever in your debt."

Sighing happily, she smiled back at him.

"Let us return to London." Pressing her other hand to their joined ones, she smiled again. "There is much for us still to say to each other, but for the moment I am relieved that it is all come to an end."

Lord Winterbrook leaned forward, kissed her cheek, and then led her to the carriage. The imprint of his lips burned, sending a fire back into her heart as they shared a smile. Their struggle was over.

CHAPTER SIXTEEN

Felix had arrived at the park much too early. Lady Elizabeth was not meant to be arriving until three in the afternoon, and he had been there from a little after two. After the excitement of the previous adventure, which had taken place only two days prior, he had allowed himself a day simply to rest. Lady Elizabeth had been busy with Lady Yardley, writing 'The London Ledger', including an article about the highwaymen and their experience of them. The publication was due to be placed out in society this very afternoon, and Felix would be one of the first to read it, but that was not what filled his thoughts. There was much he had to talk to Lady Elizabeth about, still so much yet to explain, so much he had to ask forgiveness for. Her willingness to meet him was incredible in itself, and he could not admire her more for all that she had done.

His thoughts ran back to when he had gone in search of Stafford, praying that the man would see him as vulnerable and hopeless. It had been greatly disconcerting pretending to do all that Stafford had wanted, pretending that he had no other choice but to give in. It had all been part of the charade, of course, and Stafford had been delighted that Felix had agreed to do everything which was required. How fiercely Felix's heart had beaten when he had ridden out after the carriage – a carriage which he knew contained Lady Elizabeth. It had not been with the thrill of the chase, nor with the delight of his endeavors, but rather out of fear. He had been afraid that something would go wrong, and that Lady Elizabeth might find herself in even greater danger than before.

But now, all was well.

And I can only look to Lady Elizabeth, for it is her that I have to thank for it all.

"And if she will offer me another opportunity to regain her trust, then I will grasp it with both hands."

"There you are."

Felix turned around quickly, having been so lost in his thoughts and his murmurings that he had not even noticed the arrival of Lady Elizabeth. A flush rose to his face at her presence, for her beauty and gentle smile overwhelmed him.

"I do hope that you are pleased to see me?"

With a smile, he nodded.

"I could not be more delighted." Grasping her hand, he bowed over it again, kissing the back of it as he had done so many times before. When she smiled, it dazzled him. It was brighter than the day, bringing him more warmth than the heat of the sun. She bloomed brighter than every other flower within the park, her beauty overwhelming him in a way that it had never done before. It was as if he were seeing her for the first time, as if he were looking at her with fresh eyes. How he prayed that she would not step away from him now, even though she had every reason to do so. "Shall we walk?"

She nodded, glancing over her shoulder at her mother, who was descending from the carriage.

"My mother states that she will walk a little behind us." Tilting her head, Lady Elizabeth smiled up at him again. "I did not think that we would be walking particularly quickly, however. There is much we need to say, I think."

Felix managed a brief smile, his stomach twisting this way and that as he thought of all of the things he wished to say. He would walk at a very slow pace indeed if he had to, simply so that he would give himself the time to say everything he desired.

"You are willing to listen to me, I hope?"

Lady Elizabeth fell into step beside him.

"I am."

"Then I thank you for that." Turning his head, he looked into her eyes. "I think you the most marvelous creature, Lady Elizabeth. My admiration for you could not be greater. The way you came up with the solution to my difficulties – difficulties which I had brought upon myself - is more than extraordinary to me. You did not stay back in your townhouse, even though I begged you to. Your courage would not permit you to step away, I think."

"No, indeed." Lady Elizabeth turned her head away, looking at the path rather than at him. "I certainly would not allow my friends to put themselves in danger while I remained at home. Besides, I would have been far too anxious had I remained at home." Her gaze sought his again. "I could not have borne it, waiting to know the outcome, desperate to know if you were safe and had been freed from their clutches."

Felix blinked, a sudden thrill of hope rousing fresh

energy within him.

"You care for me still?"

He did not expect Lady Elizabeth to laugh in response to his question. Her eyes twinkled, her lips lifting into a beautiful smile which forced him to respond in kind.

"Oh, my dear Lord Winterbrook, can you doubt it?" Laughing gently, she tucked her arm through his, pulling herself as close as she could. "I care for you a great deal, Lord Winterbrook. I believe that I have already told you that my affections are engaged with yours."

"But after all that I have done, after all the secrets which I kept from you, I was afraid that you might...."

"No, I have not decided against our betrothal." Lady Elizabeth smiled quietly, her voice softening. "After I first learned the truth, I believed that my heart was quite broken, and that there could be no more affection for you within it, as though it had trickled out through the wound. But very soon, I learned that it was still there, as steadfast as ever. Although," she finished, tilting her head towards him, her eyes searching his face, "I do not fully understand why you became a highwayman in the first place. What was it about the life that drew you to it? Everyone knows that you are a wealthy fellow, so surely it cannot have been because of that."

Felix shook his head.

"Certainly, it was not." Sighing, he ignored the urge to hold the truth back from her. "It is because I was selfish, as I believe I have told you. I began the Season determined to be bored by it. I told Lord Bramwell as much, stating that it was all the same as it had always been and that I desired something more to enliven me. Instead of considering what I might truly need – which I now see was a lady of quality whom I could call my own, whom I could pour my affections and consideration into - I decided that I required some sort of entertainment. I was already dulled by the idea of gambling and cards, and thus I considered that being a highwayman, for a short time, would be an excellent venture for me. Hiding my face, I went in search of three men to ride with me, for I knew that I would never be able to convince any gentleman to join me! I wanted it to be my secret undertaking for my own enjoyment, and I will admit that there *was* a good deal of excitement."

"But there was a great deal of risk also."

"Indeed, there was," Felix agreed quietly. "But I did not allow myself to even consider that. Rather, I believe that it was all part of the enjoyment. It was only when I met you, and became quite caught up with you, that the experience no longer felt as joyous as before." Lady Elizabeth was no longer smiling. She turned her head away, her gaze to the path, and together they walked in silence for some minutes. Felix wished that he could find something more to say, something which would break through the guilt which filled him still, knowing how much he had shamed himself in her eyes. "You may call me a fool if you wish, for that is precisely what I was." Speaking honestly, he walked with his gaze straight forward, not looking at her. "When I met you, my considerations began to change. It was then that I found myself doing good, rather than stealing from those I stopped. That was never my intention. I never deliberately set out to do so, but it came upon me, and I could not escape from it. I believe that it was all your influence, Lady Elizabeth."

"I do not know how you could say that it was I who did such a thing." Still, she did not smile, but there was a gentleness to her tone. "In a way, I am glad to hear that you have done some good. It is because of you that Lord Bramwell and Miss Whitford are to marry, which is truly wonderful news. It would not have taken place had you not introduced them."

"Mayhap." He shrugged. "When I first directed Miss Whitford and her granduncle to my townhouse, I secretly hoped that such a thing would happen. I am very glad to see that it has. I know that Lord Bramwell is an excellent gentleman, and he will be an exceptional husband, I am sure."

"Just as I am sure *you* shall be."

Her words were so quietly whispered that for a moment, Felix was not certain that he had heard them correctly. He kept walking, his gaze steady until the words slowly began to trickle into his mind. With a sudden, swift intake of breath, he turned sharply, only to see Lady Elizabeth smiling at him.

"Do you truly mean to say....?"

"Certainly, I do." Lady Elizabeth laughed gently, then pulled herself so close that their shoulders touched. "I have no intention of ending our betrothal, Lord Winterbrook. Indeed, I think that my heart is *more* than content to be twined with yours! I do not think that I would be able to permit myself to end what has grown between us, without severely injuring myself, and I have no desire to do such a thing as that."

Despite his attempts to speak, Felix's words tied themselves together into a ball in his throat. His chest was heaving as though he had run a great race, his heart slamming furiously within it and, as he continued to walk with Lady Elizabeth by his side, a sheen of sweat broke out across his brow - no doubt from relief and from the joy of being able to share his future with her. It was so astonishing that Felix struggled to take it in.

"You have said nothing, Lord Winterbrook." When he glanced at her, Lady Elizabeth was lifting a gentle eyebrow, though her eyes no longer held as much light as before. "I do hope that you have no intention of breaking our betrothal yourself! I hope, instead, that you are pleased."

"Pleased?" Repeating her word, Felix let out a breathless laugh and wiped one hand across his forehead. "It is impossible to express all that I feel at this moment. In truth, Lady Elizabeth, I am quite overcome."

Her eyes searched his.

"Truly?"

Swallowing hard, he nodded.

"I am fully aware that to have you as my bride is an honor which I have been blessed with, above any other gentleman. I did not truly realize its value until there was a possibility that it might fade from me. Now, it is something which I find so uplifting that it throws my heart to the sky and, as yet, it has not returned to me."

Lady Elizabeth smiled, her own sigh escaping, perhaps relieved that he had answered her in such a way. The growing desire to pull her into his arms had Felix glancing all around him, then looking over his shoulder to where Lady Longford stood. Instead of walking after them, Lady Longford had stopped and was now talking with someone else. Taking what he knew to be a great risk, he released Lady Elizabeth's hand from his arm, but rather than stepping away from her, he grasped her hand tightly in his.

"Come with me." A small copse of trees to his left offered him the perfect hiding place, and he made for it quickly, with Lady Elizabeth giggling as she followed him. There was only one desire within his heart, one urge which he could not release himself from. Had they been elsewhere, perhaps in his townhouse or Lady Elizabeth's home, then he might have found a way to give them a few minutes alone, but here, it was a good deal more difficult. Heedless as to whether or not anyone could spy them through the branches, he grasped Lady Elizabeth's hand, then bent to one knee, the small twigs cracking under him. "My darling Lady Elizabeth." Her laughing smile faded into tenderness. "I swear to you here and now, I shall do everything in my power to honor you above all else, to show you each day how much my heart yearns for you, how much it loves you, and how much affection it holds for you." Tilting his head back, Felix looked up at her, his gaze steady. "I love you, Elizabeth. I love you desperately. I can offer you nothing but myself, as foolish and as weak as I am. I want to spend every day in your company, speaking with you, drawing near you, dancing the waltz with you whenever you wish it." Lady Elizabeth's gentle laugh made him smile, though he had more to say, his fingers pressing hers. "I will not neglect this second opportunity I have been given to prove myself to you. There will never be any secrets between us for you know everything about me now. There is nothing else for me to hold back." One shoulder lifted. "I shall be the very best husband I can be, Lady Elizabeth, and I shall always be aware of the blessing which is mine in having you as my wife."

"I am not your wife yet, Lord Winterbrook, though I cannot pretend that I do not desire to hold that title soon."

Lady Elizabeth smiled gently, her cheeks a soft pink as he rose to his feet. His hands took hers and he looked into her eyes, marveling all over again at just how wonderful a creature stood before him.

"I do not think that I would know how to live without you." A dull ache settled in his heart at even the thought of being separated from her, even though he knew that there was no threat of it any longer. "I promised myself that, should you choose to end our betrothal, I would be content to step away, aware that you deserve to do just as you please. But in truth, I would have been a shadow, a mist which forms early on a summer's morning, lost to the wind."

Her hand tugged from his, reaching up to press against his cheek.

"It is just as well that I have decided that my heart loves you so dearly that it cannot be parted from you." Her eyes were full of him, her lips parting gently. "I love you, Lord Winterbrook."

Felix's heart threw itself to the skies once more. His hand released hers and he moved it to settle around her waist. The sweetness of her smile was answer enough, but when he lowered his head, he waited for her to tip her face towards him in silent answer to his question. When their lips met, it was as though his world exploded with the joy of it. Everything was a little brighter, a little more colorful, and all the more joyous. Careful not to overwhelm her with his passion, he slanted his head a little, allowing their kiss to deepen, and then slowly, reluctantly, pulled away.

"And as for myself, my dear Elizabeth," he murmured, smiling gently against her lips. "I love you too."

I LOVE a good happy ever after! I knew he would turn out to be a very good gentleman and Felix and Elizabeth are very happy!

DID you miss the first book in the **Only for Love** series? The Heart of a Gentleman Read ahead for a sneak peek!

MY DEAR READER

Thank you for reading and supporting my books! I hope this story brought you some escape from the real world into the always captivating Regency world. A good story, especially one with a happy ending, just brightens your day and makes you feel good! If you enjoyed the book, would you leave a review on Amazon? Reviews are always appreciated.

Below is a complete list of all my books! Why not click and see if one of them can keep you entertained for a few hours?

The Duke's Daughters Series
The Duke's Daughters: A Sweet Regency Romance Boxset
A Rogue for a Lady
My Restless Earl
Rescued by an Earl
In the Arms of an Earl
The Reluctant Marquess (Prequel)

A Smithfield Market Regency Romance
The Smithfield Market Romances: A Sweet Regency Romance Boxset
The Rogue's Flower
Saved by the Scoundrel
Mending the Duke
The Baron's Malady

The Returned Lords of Grosvenor Square
The Returned Lords of Grosvenor Square: A Regency Romance Boxset
The Waiting Bride
The Long Return
The Duke's Saving Grace
A New Home for the Duke

The Spinsters Guild
The Spinsters Guild: A Sweet Regency Romance Boxset
A New Beginning
The Disgraced Bride
A Gentleman's Revenge
A Foolish Wager
A Lord Undone

Convenient Arrangements
Convenient Arrangements: A Regency Romance Collection
A Broken Betrothal
In Search of Love
Wed in Disgrace
Betrayal and Lies
A Past to Forget
Engaged to a Friend

Landon House
Landon House: A Regency Romance Boxset
Mistaken for a Rake
A Selfish Heart
A Love Unbroken
A Christmas Match
A Most Suitable Bride

An Expectation of Love

Second Chance Regency Romance
Second Chance Regency Romance Boxset
Loving the Scarred Soldier
Second Chance for Love
A Family of her Own
A Spinster No More

Soldiers and Sweethearts
To Trust a Viscount
Whispers of the Heart
Dare to Love a Marquess
Healing the Earl
A Lady's Brave Heart

Ladies on their Own: Governesses and Companions
Ladies on their Own Boxset
More Than a Companion
The Hidden Governess
The Companion and the Earl
More than a Governess
Protected by the Companion

Lost Fortunes, Found Love
A Viscount's Stolen Fortune
For Richer, For Poorer
Her Heart's Choice
A Dreadful Secret
Their Forgotten Love
His Convenient Match

Only for Love

The Heart of a Gentleman
A Lord or a Liar
The Earl's Unspoken Love
The Viscount's Unlikely Ally
The Highwayman's Hidden Heart

Christmas Stories
Love and Christmas Wishes: Three Regency Romance Novellas
A Family for Christmas
Mistletoe Magic: A Regency Romance
Heart, Homes & Holidays: A Sweet Romance Anthology

Christmas Kisses Series
The Lady's Christmas Kiss
The Viscount's Christmas Queen
Her Christmas Duke

Happy Reading!
   All my love,
   Rose

A SNEAK PEEK OF THE HEART OF A GENTLEMAN

CHAPTER ONE

"Thank you again for sponsoring me through this Season." Lady Cassandra Chilton pressed her hands together tightly, a delighted smile spreading across her features as excitement quickened her heart. Having spent a few years in London, with the rest of her family, it was now finally her turn to come out into society. "I would not have been able to come to London had you not been so generous."

Norah, Lady Yardley smiled softly and slipped her arm through Cassandra's.

"I am just as glad as you to have you here, cousin." A small sigh slipped from her, and her expression was gentle. "It does not seem so long ago that I was here myself, to make my Come Out."

Cassandra's happiness faded just a little

"Your first marriage was not of great length, I recall." Pressing her lips together immediately, she winced, dropping her head, hugely embarrassed by her own forthrightness "Forgive me. I ought not to be speaking of such things."

Thankfully, Lady Yardley chuckled.

"You need not be so concerned, my dear. You are right to say that my first marriage was not of long duration, but I *have* found a great happiness since then - more than that, in fact. I have found a love which has brought me such wondrous contentment that I do not think I should ever have been able to live without it." At this, Cassandra found herself sighing softly, her eyes roving around the London streets as though they might land on the very gentleman who would thereafter bring her the same love, within her own heart, that her cousin spoke of. "But you must be cautious," her cousin continued. "There are many gentlemen in London – even more during the Season – and not *all* of them will seek the same sort of love match as you. Therefore, you must always be cautious, my dear."

A little surprised at this, Cassandra looked at her cousin as they walked along the London streets.

"I must be cautious?"

Her cousin nodded sagely.

"Yes, most careful, my dear. Society is not always as it appears. It can be a fickle friend." Lady Yardley glanced at Cassandra then quickly smiled - a smile which Cassandra did not immediately believe. "Pray, do not allow me to concern you, not when you have only just arrived in London!" She shook her head and let out an exasperated sigh, evidently directed towards herself. "No doubt you will have a wonderful Season. With so much to see and to enjoy, I am certain that these months will be delightful."

Cassandra allowed herself a small smile, her shoulders relaxing in gentle relief. She had always assumed that London society would be warm and welcoming and, whilst there was always the danger of scandal, that danger came only from young ladies or gentlemen choosing to behave improperly. Given that she was quite determined *not* to behave so, there could be no danger of scandal for her!

"I assure you, Norah, that I shall be impeccable in my behavior and in my speech. You need not concern yourself over that."

Lady Yardley touched her hand for a moment.

"I am sure that you shall. I have never once considered otherwise." She offered a quick smile. "But you will also learn a great deal about society and the gentlemen within it – and that will stand you in good stead."

Still not entirely certain, and pondering what her cousin meant, Cassandra found her thoughts turned in an entirely new direction when she saw someone she recognized. Miss Bridget Wynch was accompanied by another young lady who Cassandra knew, and with a slight squeal of excitement, she made to rush towards them – somehow managing to drag Lady Yardley with her. When Cassandra turned to apologize, her cousin laughingly disentangled herself and then urged Cassandra to continue to her friends. Cassandra did so without hesitation and, despite the fact it was in the middle of London, the three young ladies embraced each other openly, their voices high with excitement. Over the last few years, they had come to know each other as they had accompanied various elder siblings to London, alongside their parents. Now it was to be their turn and the joy of that made Cassandra's heart sing.

"You are here then, Cassandra." Lady Almeria grasped her hand tightly. "And you were so concerned that your father would not permit you to come."

"It was not that he was unwilling to permit me to attend, rather that he was concerned that he would be on the continent at the time," Cassandra explained. "In that regard, he was correct, for both my father *and* my mother have taken leave of England, and have gone to my father's properties on the continent. I am here, however, and stay now with my cousin." Turning, she gestured to Lady Yardley who was standing only a short distance away, a warm smile on her face. She did not move forward, as though she was unwilling to interrupt the conversation and, with a smile of gratitude, Cassandra turned back to her friends. "We are to make our first appearances in Society tomorrow." Stating this, she let out a slow breath. "How do you each feel?"

With a slight squeal, Miss Wynch closed her eyes and shuddered.

"Yes, we are, and I confess that I am quite terrified." Taking a breath, she pressed one hand to her heart. "I am very afraid that I will make a fool of myself in some way."

"As am I," Lady Almeria agreed. "I am afraid that I shall trip over my gown and fall face first in front of the most important people of the *ton*! Then what shall be said of me?"

"They will say that you may not be the most elegant young lady to dance with?" Cassandra suggested, as her friends giggled. "However, I am quite sure that you will have a great deal of poise – as you always do – and will be able to control your nerves quite easily. You will not so much as stumble."

"I thank you for your faith in me."

Lady Almeria let out a slow breath.

"Our other friends will be present also," Miss Wynch added. "How good it will be to see them again – both at our presentation and at the ball in the evening!"

Cassandra smiled at the thought of the ball, her stomach twisting gently with a touch of nervousness.

"I admit to being excited about our first ball also. I do

wonder which gentlemen we shall dance with." Lady Almeria swiveled her head around, looking at the many passersby before leaning forward a little more and dropping her voice low. "I am hopeful that one or two may become of significant interest to us."

Cassandra's smile fell.

"My cousin has warned me to be cautious when it comes to the gentlemen of London." Still a little disconcerted by what Lady Yardley had said to her, Cassandra gave her friends a small shrug. "I do not understand precisely what she meant, but there is something about the gentlemen of London of which we must be careful. My cousin has not explained to me precisely what that is as yet, but states that there is much I must learn. I confess to you, since we have all been in London before, for previous Seasons – albeit not for ourselves – I did not think that there would be a great deal for me to understand."

"I do not know what things Lady Yardley speaks of," Miss Wynch agreed, a small frown between her eyebrows now. "My elder sister did not have any difficulty with *her* husband. When they met, they were so delighted with each other they were wed within six weeks."

"I confess I know very little about Catherine's engagement and marriage," Lady Almeria replied, speaking of her elder sister who was some ten years her senior. "But I *do* know that Amanda had a little trouble, although I believe that came from the realization that she had to choose which gentleman was to be her suitor. She had *three* gentlemen eager to court her – all deserving gentlemen too – and therefore, she had some trouble in deciding who was best suited."

Cassandra frowned, her nose wrinkling.

"I could not say anything about my brother's marriage, but my sister did wait until her second Season before she accepted a gentleman's offer of courtship. She spoke very little to me of any difficulties, however - and therefore, I do not understand what my cousin means." A small sigh escaped her. "I do wish that my sister and I had been a little closer. She might have spoken to me of whatever difficulties she faced, whether they were large or small, but in truth, she said very little to me. Had she done so, then I might be already aware of whatever it is that Lady Yardley wishes to convey."

Miss Wynch put one hand on her arm.

"I am sure that we shall find out soon enough." She shrugged. "I do not think that you need to worry about it either, given that we have more than enough to think about! Maybe after our come out, Lady Yardley will tell you all."

Cassandra took a deep breath and let herself smile as the tension flooded out of her.

"Yes, you are right." Throwing a quick glance back towards her cousin, who was still standing nearby, she spread both hands. "Regardless of what is said, I am still determined to marry for love."

"As am I." Lady Almeria's lips tipped into a soft smile. "In fact, I think that all of us – our absent friends included – are determined to marry for love. Did we not all say so last Season, as we watched our sisters and brothers make their matches? I find myself just as resolved today as I was then. I do not think our desires a foolish endeavor."

Cassandra shook her head.

"Nor do I, although my brother would have a different opinion, given that he trumpeted how excellent a match he made with his new bride."

With a wry laugh, she tilted her head, and looked from one friend to the other.

"And my sister would have laughed at us for such a

suggestion, I confess," Lady Almeria agreed. "She states practicality to be the very best of situations, but I confess I dream of more."

"As do I." A slightly wistful expression came over Miss Wynch as she clasped both hands to her heart, her eyes closing for a moment. "I wish to know that a gentleman's heart is filled only with myself, rather than looking at me as though I am some acquisition suitable for his household."

Such a description made Cassandra shudder as she nodded fervently. To be chosen by a gentleman simply due to her father's title, or for her dowry, would be most displeasing. To Cassandra's mind, it would not bring any great happiness.

"Then I have a proposal." Cassandra held out her hands, one to each of her friends. "What say you we promise each other – here and now, that we shall *only* marry for love and shall support each other in our promises to do so? We can speak to our other friends and seek their agreement also."

Catching her breath, Lady Almeria nodded fervently, her smile spreading across her face.

"It sounds like a wonderful idea."

"I quite agree." Miss Wynch smiled back at her, reaching to grasp Cassandra's hand. "We shall speak to the others soon, I presume?"

"Yes, of course. We shall have a merry little band together and, in time, we are certain to have success." Cassandra sighed contentedly, the last flurries of tension going from her. "We will all find ourselves suitable matches with gentlemen to whom we can lose our hearts, knowing that their hearts love us in return."

As her friends smiled, Cassandra's heart began to soar. This Season was going to be an excellent one, she was sure.

Yes, she had her cousin's warnings, but she also had her friends' support in her quest to find a gentleman who would love her; a gentleman she would carry in her heart for all of her days. Surely such a fellow would not be so difficult to find?

CHAPTER TWO

"*I* should like to hear something... significant... about you this Season."

Jonathan rolled his eyes, knowing precisely what his mother expected. This was now his fourth Season in London and, as yet, he had not found himself a bride – much to his mother's chagrin, of course. On his part, it was quite deliberate and, although he had stated as much to his mother on various occasions, it did not seem to alter her attempts to encourage him toward matrimony.

"You are aware that you did not have to come to London with me, Mother?" Jonathan shrugged his shoulders. "If you had remained at home, then you would not have suffered as much concern, surely?"

"It is a legitimate concern, which I would suffer equally, no matter where I am!" his mother shot back fiercely. "You have not given me any expectation of a forthcoming marriage and I continually wonder and worry over the lack of an heir! You are the Marquess of Sherbourne! You have responsibilities!"

Jonathan scowled.

"Responsibilities I take seriously, Mother. However, I will not be forced into–"

"I have already heard whispers of your various entanglements during last Season. I can hardly imagine that this Season will be any better."

At this, Jonathan took a moment to gather himself, trying to control the fierce surge of anger now burning in his soul. When he spoke, it was with a quietness he could barely keep hold of.

"I assure you, such whispers have been greatly exaggerated. I am not a scoundrel."

He could tell immediately that this did not please his mother, for she shook her head and let out a harsh laugh.

"I do not believe that," she stated, her tone still fierce. "Especially when my *dear* friend, Lady Edmonds, tells me that you were attempting to entice her daughter into your arms!" Her eyes closed tight. "The fact that she is still willing to even be my friend is very generous indeed."

A slight pang of guilt edged into Jonathan's heart, but he ignored it with an easy shrug of his shoulders.

"Do you truly think that Lady Hannah was so unwilling? That I had to coerce her somehow?" Seeing how his mother pressed one hand to her mouth, he rolled his eyes for the second time. "It is the truth I tell you, Mother. Whether you wish to believe me or not, any rumors you have heard have been greatly exaggerated. For example, Lady Hannah was the one who came to seek *me* out, rather than it being me pursuing her."

His mother rose from her chair, her chin lifting and her face a little flushed.

"I will not believe that Lady Hannah, who is so delicate a creature, would even have *dreamt* of doing such a thing as that!"

"You very may very well not believe it, and that would not surprise me, given that everyone else holds much the same opinion." Spreading both hands, Jonathan let out a small sigh. "I may not be eager to wed, Mother, but I certainly am not a scoundrel or a rogue, as you appear to believe me to be."

His mother looked away, her hands planted on her hips, and Jonathan scowled, frustrated by his mother's lack of belief in his character. During last Season, he had been utterly astonished when Lady Hannah had come to speak with him directly, only to attempt to draw him into some sort of assignation. And she only in her first year out in Society as well! Jonathan had always kept far from those young ladies who were newly out – even, as in this case, from those who had been so very obvious in their eagerness. No doubt being a little upset by his lack of willingness, Lady Hannah had gone on to tell her mother a deliberate untruth about him, suggesting that *he* had been the one to try to negotiate something warm between them. And now, it seemed, his own mother believed that same thing. It was not the first time that such rumors had been spread about gentlemen – himself included and, on some occasions, Jonathan admitted, the rumors had come about because of his actions. But other whispers, such as this, were grossly unfair. Yet who would believe the word of a supposedly roguish gentleman over that of a young lady? There was, Jonathan considered, very little point in arguing.

"I will not go near Lady Hannah this Season, if that is what is concerning you." With a slight lift of his shoulders, Jonathan tried to smile at his mother, but only received an angry glare in return. "I assure you that I have no interest in Lady Hannah! She is not someone I would consider even stepping out with, were I given the opportunity." Protesting his innocence was futile, he knew, but yet the words kept coming. "I do not even think her overly handsome."

"Are you stating that she is ugly?"

Jonathan closed his eyes, stifling a groan. It seemed that he could say nothing which would bring his mother any satisfaction. The only thing to please her would be if he declared himself betrothed to a suitable young lady. At present, however, he had very little intention of doing anything of the sort. He was quite content with his life, such as it was. The time to continue the family line would come soon enough, but he could give it a few more years until he had to consider it.

"No, mother, Lady Hannah is not ugly." Seeing how her frown lifted just a little, he took his opportunity to escape. "Now, if you would excuse me, I have an afternoon tea to attend." His mother's eyebrows lifted with evident hope, but Jonathan immediately set her straight. "With Lord and Lady Yardley," he added, aware of how quickly her features slumped again. "I have no doubt that you will be a little frustrated by the fact that my ongoing friendship with Lord and Lady Yardley appears to be the most significant connection in my life, but he is a dear friend and his wife has become so also. Surely you can find no complaint there!" His mother sniffed and looked away, and Jonathan, believing now that there was very little he could say to even bring a smile to his mother's face, turned his steps towards the door. "Good afternoon, Mother."

So saying, he strode from the room, fully aware of the heavy weight of expectation that his mother continually placed upon his shoulders. He could not give her what she wanted, and her ongoing criticism was difficult to hear. She did not have proof of his connection to Lady Hannah but, all the same, thought poorly of him. She would criticize his close acquaintance with Lord and Lady Yardley also! His friendships were quickly thrown aside, as were his explanations and his pleadings of innocence - there was nothing he could say or do that would bring her even a hint of satisfaction, and Jonathan had no doubt that, during this Season, he would be a disappointment to her all over again.

∽

"Good afternoon, Yardley."

His friend beamed at him, turning his head for a moment as he poured two measures of brandy into two separate glasses.

"Sherbourne! Good afternoon, do come in. It appears to be an excellent afternoon, does it not?"

Jonathan did so, his eyes on his friend, gesturing to the brandy on the table.

"It will more than excellent once you hand me the glass which I hope is mine."

Lord Yardley chuckled and obliged him.

"And yet, it seems as though you are troubled all the same," he remarked, as Jonathan took a sip of what he knew to be an excellent French brandy. "Come then, what troubles you this time?" Lifting an eyebrow, he grinned as Jonathan groaned aloud. "I am certain it will have something to do with your dear mother."

Letting out an exasperated breath, Jonathan gesticulated in the air as Lord Yardley took a seat opposite him.

"She wishes me to be just as you are." Jonathan took a small sip of his brandy. "Whereas I am less and less inclined to wed myself to *any* young lady who has her approval... simply because she will have my mother's approval!"

Lord Yardley chuckled and then took a sip from his

glass.

"That is difficult indeed! You are quite right to state that *you* will be the one to decide when you wed… so long as it is not simply because you are avoiding your responsibilities."

"I am keenly aware of my responsibilities, which is precisely *why* I avoid matrimony. I already have a great deal of demands on my time – I can only imagine that to add a wife to that burden would only increase it!"

"You are quite mistaken."

Jonathan chuckled darkly.

"You only say so because your wife is an exceptional lady. I think you one of the *few* gentlemen who finds themselves so blessed."

Lord Yardley shrugged.

"Then I must wonder if you believe the state of matrimony to be a death knell to a gentleman's heart. I can assure you it is quite the opposite."

"You say that only because you have found contentment," Jonathan shot back quickly. "There are many gentlemen who do not find themselves so comfortable."

Lord Yardley shrugged.

"There may be more than you know." He picked up his brandy glass again. "And if that is what you seek from your forthcoming marriage to whichever young lady you choose, then why do you not simply search for a suitable match, rather than doing very little other than entertain yourself throughout the Season? You could find a lady who would bring you a great deal of contentment, I am sure."

Resisting the urge to roll his eyes, Jonathan spread both hands, one still clutching his brandy, the other one empty.

"Because I do not feel the same urgency about the matter as my mother," he stated firmly. "When the time is right, I will find an excellent young lady who will fill my heart with such great affection that I will be unable to do anything but look into her eyes and find myself lost. *Then* I will know that she is the one I ought to wed. However, until that moment comes, I will continue on, just as I am at present." For a moment he thought that his friend would laugh at him, but much to his surprise, Lord Yardley simply nodded in agreement. There was not even a hint of a smile on his lips, but rather a gentle understanding in his eyes which spoke of acceptance of all that Jonathan had said. "Let us talk of something other than my present situation." Throwing back the rest of his brandy, and with a great and contented sigh, Jonathan set the glass back down on the table to his right. "Your other guests have not arrived as yet, I see. Are you hoping for a jovial afternoon?"

"A cheerful afternoon, certainly, although we will not be overwhelmed by too many guests today." Lord Yardley grinned. "It is a little unfortunate that I shall soon have to return to my estate." His smile faded a little. "I do not like the idea of being away from my wife, but there are many improvements taking place at the estate which must be overseen." His lips pulled to one side for a moment. "Besides which, my wife has her cousin to chaperone this Season."

"Her cousin?" Repeating this, Jonathan frowned as his friend nodded. "You did not mention this to me before."

"Did I not?" Lord Yardley replied mildly, waving one hand as though it did not matter. "Yes, my wife is to be chaperoning her cousin for the duration of the Season. The girl's parents are both on the continent, you understand, and given that she would not have much of a coming out otherwise, my wife thought it best to offer."

Jonathan tried to ignore the frustration within him at the fact that his friend would not be present for the Season, choosing instead to nod.

"How very kind of her. And what is the name of this cousin?"

"Lady Cassandra Chilton." Lord Yardley's gaze flew towards the door. "No doubt you will meet her this afternoon. I do not know what is taking them so long but, then again, I have never been a young lady about to make her first appearance in Society."

Jonathan blinked. Clearly this was more than just an afternoon tea. This Lady Cassandra would be present this afternoon so that she might become acquainted with a few of those within society. Why Lord Yardley had not told him about this before, Jonathan did not know – although it was very like his friend to forget about such details.

"Lady Cassandra is being presented this afternoon?"

His friend nodded.

"Yes, as we speak. I did offer to go with them, of course, but was informed she was already nervous enough, and would be quite contented with just my dear wife standing beside her."

Jonathan nodded and was about to make some remark about how difficult a moment it must be for a young lady to be presented to the Queen, only for the door to open and Lady Yardley herself to step inside.

"Ah, Lord Sherbourne. How delighted I am to see you."

With a genuine smile on her face, she waved at him to remain seated rather than attempt to get up to greet her.

"Good afternoon, Lady Yardley. I do hope the presentation went well?"

"Exceptionally well. Cassandra has just gone up to change out of her presentation gown – those gowns which the Queen requires are so outdated and uncomfortable! She will join us shortly."

The lady threw a broad smile in the direction of her

husband, who then rose immediately from his chair to go towards her. Taking her hands, he pressed a kiss to the back of one and then to the back of the other. It was a display of affection usually reserved only for private moments, but Jonathan was well used to such things between Lord and Lady Yardley. In many ways, he found it rather endearing.

"I am sure that Cassandra did very well with you beside her."

Lady Yardley smiled at her husband.

"She has a great deal of strength," she replied, quietly. "I find her quite remarkable. Indeed, I was proud to be there beside her."

"I have only just been hearing about your cousin, Lady Yardley. I do hope to be introduced to her very soon." Shifting in his chair, Jonathan waved his empty glass at Lord Yardley, who laughed but went in search of the brandy regardless. "You are sponsoring her through the Season, I understand."

His gaze now fixed itself on Lady Yardley, aware of that soft smile on her face.

"Yes, I am." Settling herself in her chair, she let out a small sigh as she did so. "I have no doubt that she will be a delight to society. She is young and beautiful and very well-considered, albeit a little naïve."

A slight frown caught Jonathan's forehead.

"Naïve?"

Lady Yardley nodded.

"Yes, just as every young lady new to society has been, and will be for years to come. She is quite certain that she will find herself hopelessly in love with the very best of a gentleman and that he will seek to marry her by the end of the Season."

"Such things do happen, my dear."

Lady Yardley laughed softly at Lord Yardley's remark, reaching across from her chair to grasp her husband's hand.

"I am not saying that they do not, only that my dear cousin thinks that all will be marvelously well for her in society and that the *ton* is a welcoming creature rather than one to be most cautious of. I, however, am much more on my guard. Not every gentleman who seeks her out will be looking to marry her. Not every gentleman who seeks her out will believe in the concept of love."

"Love?" Jonathan snorted, rolling his eyes to himself as both Lord and Lady Yardley turned their attention towards him. Flushing, he shrugged. "I suppose I would count myself as someone who does not believe such a thing to have any importance. I may not even believe in the concept!"

Lady Yardley's eyes opened wide.

"You mean to say that what Lord Yardley and I share is something you do not believe in?"

Blinking rapidly, Jonathan tried to explain, his chest suddenly tight.

"No, it is not that I do not believe it a meaningful connection which can be found between two people such as yourselves. It is that I personally have no interest in it. I have no intention of marrying someone simply because I find myself in love with them. In truth, I do not know if I am even capable of such a feeling."

"I can assure you that you are, whether or not you believe yourself to be."

Lord Yardley muttered his remark rather quietly and Jonathan took in a slow breath, praying that his friend would not start instructing him on the matter of love."

Lady Yardley smiled and gazed at Jonathan for some moments before taking a breath and continuing.

"All the same, I do want my cousin to be cautious, particularly during this evening's ball. I want her to understand that not every gentleman will be as she expects."

"I am sure such gentlemen will make that obvious all by themselves."

This brought a frown to Lady Yardley's features, but a chuckle came from Lord Yardley instead. Jonathan grinned, just as the door opened and a young lady stepped into the room, beckoned by Lady Yardley. A gentle smile softened her delicate features as she glanced around the room, her eyes finally lingering on Jonathan.

"I feel as though I have walked into something most mysterious since everyone stopped talking the moment I entered." One eyebrow arching, she smiled at him. "I do hope that someone will tell me what it is all about!"

Jonathan rose, as was polite, but his lips seemed no longer able to deliver speech. Even his breath seemed to have fixed itself inside his chest as he stared, his mouth ajar, at the beautiful young woman who had just walked in. Her skin was like alabaster, her lips a gentle pink, pulled into a soft smile as blue eyes sparkled back at him. He had nothing to say and everything to say at the very same time. Could this delightful young woman be Lady Yardley's cousin? And if she was, then why was no one introducing him?

"Allow me to introduce you." As though he had read his thoughts, Lord Yardley threw out one hand towards the young woman. "Might I present Lady Cassandra, daughter to the Earl of Holford. And this, Lady Cassandra, is my dear friend, the Marquess of Sherbourne. He is an excellent sort. You need have no fears with him."

Bowing quickly towards the young woman, Jonathan fought to find his breath.

"I certainly would not be so self-aggrandizing as to say

that I was 'an excellent sort', Lady Cassandra." he was somehow unable to draw his gaze away from her, and his heart leaped in his chest when she smiled all the more. "But I shall be the most excellent companion to you, should you require it, just as I am with Lord and Lady Yardley."

There was a breath of silence, and Jonathan cleared his throat, aware that he had just said more to her than he had ever said to any other young lady upon first making their acquaintance. Even Lord Yardley appeared to be a little surprised, for there was a blink, a smile and, after another long pause, the conversation continued. Lady Yardley gestured for her cousin to come and sit beside her, and the young lady obliged. Jonathan finally managed to drag his eyes away to another part of the room, only just becoming aware of how frantically his heart was beating. Everything he had just said to his friend regarding what would occur should he ever meet a young lady who stole his attention in an instant came back to him. Had he meant those words?

Giving himself a slight shake, Jonathan settled back into his chair, lost in thought as conversation flowed around the room. This was nothing more than an instant attraction, the swift kick of desire which would be gone within a few hours. There was nothing of any seriousness in such a swift response, he told himself. He had nothing to concern himself with and thus, he tried to insert himself back into the conversation just as quickly as he could.

Oh, no, Jonathan likes her! Perhaps he will have to change his mind about becoming leg-shackled! Check out the rest of story in the Kindle Store The Heart of a Gentleman

JOIN MY MAILING LIST

Sign up for my newsletter to stay up to date on new releases, contests, giveaways, freebies, and deals!

Free book with signup!

Monthly Facebook Giveaways! Books and Amazon gift cards!
Join me on Facebook: https://www.facebook.com/rosepearsonauthor

Website: www.RosePearsonAuthor.com

Follow me on Goodreads: Author Page

Printed in Great Britain
by Amazon